THE CHRISTMAS CALLS

This is a work of fiction. Names, characters, places, and incidents are either the product of the author's imagination or are used fictitiously. Any resemblance to actual events, locales, organizations, or persons living or dead is entirely coincidental and beyond the intent of either the author or publisher.

THE CHRISTMAS CALLS

First edition. December 2022.

Copyright © 2022 Timi Petal/Lovely Petal Books

Editor: Brooke De Lira

ISBN: 979-8-9855366-2-1

The Christmas Calls

Timi Petal

DEDICATION

I'd like to thank my wonderful family for always believing in me and letting me chase my dreams. I love you all.

DECEMBER 2017

Chapter 1

Elliot

Delicate flakes fell from the sky, blanketing the ground below. The frosty winter air was priming the eight hundred inhabitants of Shadow Birch, Vermont for the upcoming holiday season. The streets and quaint shops were already decked out in festive decorations, but the snow tied everything together. Since the town was relatively small, the council, always decided on a theme a few months beforehand so everyone could join in on the festivities. This year, they went with the classics. Anything red and green, maybe even a hint of white and gold with decorations that harken back to times of antiquity.

Elliot loved his hometown, but sometimes the holiday festivities were a bit much especially at Christmas. He didn't dislike the holiday, but having spent his whole life living the same small-town routine, it got a little redundant. To make matters worse, his father left his small coffee shop to him in his will. That meant Elliot didn't have to decorate only his house, but the shop too. By the time he got done with the two, he was usually sick of seeing all the decorations around town.

As Elliot hung up the final piece of his Christmas display, a sigh of relief left his lips. This last touch was a modest wreath that hung on the glass door, right outside the shop. He was happy that the theme was simple this year. Not that he didn't have an overflowing stash of holiday decorations that could match almost any theme these days. But at least this way, he didn't have to make an elaborate plan to coordinate with it. He looked things over a few times, making sure the lights worked and the wreath wasn't crooked, before heading back inside.

Astrid, one of his four employees, was sweeping the gray laminate floor to get ready to open up shop. Her fire-red hair that tumbled past her shoulder blades swayed as she worked. She paused mid-sweep and said to Elliot, "You could have waited until Matt came in."

"I'd rather do it myself. Besides, Matt always gets here late, and I don't need him disturbing our customers by stringing lights over their heads," Elliot said.

"You mean our five returning patrons, and those occasional lone guests driving through?"

"Okay, so we're never exactly filled to capacity. But you know I have a certain way of doing things."

She smirked. "Believe me, I am well aware. I may have only worked with your father for a few years before he passed, but I distinctly remember he was the same way."

Elliot smiled to himself. "Yeah, I guess we always had that in common. We weren't ones to hand the reins off to someone else. My mother always hated that. Especially after that one time my father decided to fix our broken oven himself on Thanksgiving Day. We wound up having to use the ovens here instead."

Astrid nodded knowingly. "I remember your dad telling me that story. He said that he never tried to fix another appliance again."

"Nope, and he stuck to his word."

Astrid went back to sweeping and said, "Well, I guess I'll finish this up."

"All right. We don't want to keep our five guests waiting," he said with a chuckle.

She giggled back as she swept the dust into a neat pile. Meanwhile, Elliot walked back to the kitchen and started gathering the supplies they needed for the day. He set up all the machines, placed the pastries in the glass display at the front counter, and made sure everything was in order. The back door swung open, and a young man in his early twenties scurried inside. He threw his navy-blue coat onto one of the five coat hooks in the back. As he tossed some of his smaller items into a black cubby underneath the coat hooks, Elliot chided, "You're late, Matt."

"I won't let it happen again," Matt said.

Elliot shook his head, casting him a glare. "You say that every day."

"This time I mean it."

Astrid walked to the back to stow the broom and chimed in, "No, he doesn't. He'll be here around opening, like always."

Matt scoffed. "I won't. You'll see. From here on out, I'm going to start coming in on time."

Elliot placed a hand on Matt's shoulder and said, "Good. But if you don't keep your word on that, I'm going to have to fire you."

Matt gave him a pleading look. "Oh, come on, man. I need this job."

"I know, but I need you to show me that you're motivated."

He nodded, holding his chin higher. "Fine, I can do that."

Astrid walked by and said to Matt, "He's not going to fire you. He's been threatening you with that line for a year now."

Elliot glared at his more dependable employee and asked, "How many times have I threatened to fire *you*?"

"Never."

"Well, consider this your first. Now, go manage the cash register," he said with a joking smirk before turning to Matt. "And you, go turn the sign around and unlock the front door. We don't want our customers standing out in the cold."

Matt sauntered away, and Elliot retreated to his small office to put away some stray decorations he didn't end up using. While stuffing them in his supply closet, the phone at his desk rang. He huffed as he pushed the mountain of items flooding his closet further back so he could close the door. It was a struggle, but he eventually got it to latch shut. He jogged over to his desk as the phone went to its third ring and answered with a breathless, "Hello."

"I need to take the day off today, Elliot," his employee, Andrew, said on the other end.

He rubbed his forehead with a sigh. "Okay . . . I guess I can ask Rosaline to come in."

"I'm sorry, boss. My son has a fever, and now I feel like I'm coming down with a little something."

"No, no. Don't worry about it. Take care of yourself and Anthony." He sighed as he remembered Andrew's husband and daughter. "How are Paul and India?"

"Paul's still in Brazil for his business trip. India seems fine, so I sent her off to school."

"Great to hear. So, when can I expect to see you in again?"

"I'm hoping in a couple of days. I'll let you know on Sunday."

Elliot nodded to himself. "Sounds good. I hope you both feel better soon."

"Thanks, boss. Talk to you soon."

He hung up before ringing his last employee, Rosaline. It rung twice before a sweet older voice answered the phone.

"Hello, Rosaline. This is Elliot Lawson, your boss," he said.

She let out a light chuckle and said, "I know who you are, dear. I'm not *that* old."

Elliot felt his face warm. "Sorry about that."

"Do you need me to come in?"

"I do. Andrew and his son Anthony are sick."

"Oh, that's awful. I'll be there in a jiff."

Elliot breathed a sigh of relief. "Thank you, Rosaline. I'll see you soon."

After hanging up, he walked out to the front of the café. Two of their regulars were already in their respective seats, eating their pastries and drinking their coffee. One was the old man who lived three doors down from him, Mr. Reinhart. The other was Sophia Nolan, his ex-girlfriend and one of the two dentists in town, the second being her father, Joel Nolan. Elliot wasn't a brace-faced teenager anymore, but the man still terrified him. Mr. Nolan had never approved of his and Sophia's relationship, and even now, he doubted the man would ever warm up to him.

From the corner of his eye, Elliot glimpsed Astrid tying her hair into a bun as she made her way over to him. "I see you staring, Mr. Lawson."

He rolled his eyes, peeling them away from Sophia to look at Astrid. "I was just looking over the place."

"Sure . . . I've seen you scan the room before, and you were pausing much longer than necessary. Your eyes were totally lingering on your ex."

Elliot propped his hands on his hips. "Don't you have work to do?"

"If you were surveying the place like you say you were, you'd notice there isn't much to do."

He narrowed his eyes as he looked at his smirking employee. "Fine. So, I still have some feelings for her, but they're friendly. She's dating Hudson Marlow anyway. In fact, I think they just got engaged."

She patted her boss's back and said, "I forgot she was with that brainless piece of meat. He's sweet but doesn't know what planet he's on."

"That's true, but they seem happy together. And I'm happy for her."

Sophia turned in her chair, peering at the two with a raised brow. "You know I can hear you, right?"

Astrid snickered as she wandered back to the cash register while Elliot walked over to Sophia. He tried to put on his most charming grin and said, "I didn't think you could."

"This place is as small as the inside of a shoebox. It's hard to miss conversations."

Elliot frowned. "Right . . . Sorry about dissing Hudson."

"It's fine. It is true though. My fiancé isn't the brightest man in the world, but he makes up for it with his pleasant demeanor."

"He is a big teddy bear. I remember how he used to rescue cats and pick dandelions for our teachers and moms back in middle school."

She tucked a stray wisp of blond hair behind her ear. "Have you started seeing anyone?"

Elliot scratched at the back of his neck, as he thought of how to answer. He was hoping to avoid this question, but here it was. He shook his head as he dropped his hand and answered as truthfully as he could. "There hasn't been much time. I've been busy taking care of the café and what not. It's just not at the forefront of my mind."

"I understand. It doesn't help that this is a small town. We've grown up with practically everyone here."

"That too."

Her cell phone buzzed, and she checked the message that popped up. With a sigh, she said, "I hate to run, but I have a root canal to perform in fifteen minutes."

He forced a smile. "Not a problem. I'll clear the table for you."

"Thank you, Elliot. I'll see you tomorrow."

Sophia stood from her seat, planting a quick kiss on his stubbled cheek before leaving the café. He threw her used napkin in the trash and carried her empty coffee mug to the commercial sink in the kitchen. His office was right next to the kitchen, so he could hear the faint ring of his phone. Making his way to the adjacent room, he picked up the phone with all the professionalism he could manage.

"Lawson's Bistro. How may I help you?"

"Do you have any of those pintsized chocolate chip cookies?" a familiar female voice asked.

"We may have a few, but you have to get here before closing."

"When's that again? Six o'clock?"

He sneered playfully. "You'd know if you came around more often."

A faint chuckle rose from the other end of the line. "If work wasn't so time-consuming, I would."

"When are you coming in, Angela?" Elliot asked his older sister.

"I hope before six, because I need those cookies. I've been craving them for months."

"I could have sent you some. I think the only reason those tasteless dough bites are still being baked is because of you anyway."

She scoffed and said, "I'm sure they're loved by many while I'm out of town. Plus, they aren't the same when I don't eat them in Shadow Birch."

"Maybe two others in this town have as terrible taste buds as yours, but that's about it."

"Oh, hush. So, how have things been?"

Elliot pressed the phone to his ear with a shallow exhale. "Not bad. We're keeping the place running, so that's what matters."

"That's great and all, but I meant with you. You're not working yourself to the bone, are you?"

Elliot groaned as he leaned against his desk. "Of course not. I spend a healthy amount of time working. And I still go to the gym a few times a week on top of that."

"Good. I don't want you to consume your life with work."

Elliot smirked. "That's rich, coming from you."

"Listen, I may not be practicing what I preach, but as your older sister, I make the rules."

"I'm thirty, sis. I think I can live by my own rules now."

"Not if I can help it. Anyway, we'll catch up some more once I get up there later. I have a few things to finish up."

"Fine, I'll see you then."

He hung up and smiled down at the outdated charcoal-gray phone. Since his sister was sixteen years older than him, he had fond memories of her babysitting him while their parents worked or went out on dates. She was always telling him what to do, and as much as he despised her playful nagging, he secretly loved it too. In some ways, Angela was like a second mother, and he couldn't wait to see her for the first time in months.

Chapter 2

Autumn

Five papers with intricate drawings and designs fluttered down the sidewalk. Autumn rushed to pick them up as icy rain trickled from the sky. As she caught the last one, her phone buzzed in her tan trench coat. She sheafed together the drenched sheets of paper, trying to figure out what to do with them as she fished her phone out of her pocket with her free hand. She glanced at the name on her phone, letting out a breathless sigh before answering. "Levi, I'm right out front."

"Thank God . . . Mr. and Mrs. Peterson are getting extremely impatient. They're so close to calling Mrs. Lamour," Autumn's co-worker and best friend lamented on the other end.

"Tell them I'm here. I need to speak to you on the porch for a minute, though."

"Okay, give me a second."

Autumn hung up, stuffing her phone back into her pocket before grabbing her brown leather briefcase from her car. She quickly scurried up the walkway to the front of the newly built house, where she was met by Levi who just exited the front door. He had a giant smirk gracing his thin pink lips as he looked the disheveled woman over. She handed him the soggy papers, which wiped the grin right off his face, leaving him with a deep frown.

"Please tell me these are not the drafts for the Peterson home?" Levi asked as he peeled one of the limp documents away from another.

"Most of them. I do have some backups, but two of these now-useless papers were my main focal points."

"I guess we just have to make do with whatever you got in here. We've already pushed this project out a whole month. We can't keep them waiting any longer."

Autumn tugged back her hood and said, "What if they don't like it?"

Levi grabbed the sides of her arms and squeezed them reassuringly. "Then it's on them. I've known you since middle school, and you've always been great at making things up on the fly for school projects. After five years of working together, I know what you're capable of. You've got this, girlfriend."

She sucked in a breath of courage. "You're right. I don't need those designs to show them my vision for this place."

"That's what I like to hear. Now let's go, before they blow a fuse."

The two walked through the front door, and as soon as Autumn had her coat draped over her arm, a shrill voice said, "Ms. Burke, you had us waiting for an hour. Do you know how inconvenient that is?"

Autumn bit her tongue. Forcing herself not to snap at the older woman, she replied as professionally as she could, "I'm extremely sorry, Mrs. Peterson. I had issues with my printer while running off some copies for you, and the rain wasn't of any help getting here."

The woman jutted her chin. "Don't apologize. I just want to get this over with. We do have other things to do today."

Mr. Peterson spoke up, addressing his wife. "Vivian, leave the poor girl alone. She's trying her best."

"Well, her best simply isn't good enough. I placed her on this project because Margarete bragged to me that she was a rising talent at her company. I gave her the benefit of the doubt, but clearly I was wrong."

Her cheeks burning, Autumn placed her briefcase on the gray marble countertop of the kitchen island, avoiding eye contact with the couple. She pulled out the extra designs she had drawn of the home, grateful that they weren't destroyed by the Seattle rain. Autumn handed one of the living room designs over to Mrs. Peterson and passed another of the dining room and kitchen to her husband. The woman tilted her head as she looked over the illustration before eyeing the empty living room. She shifted her hip as she nodded slowly, as if considering the prospect. She pointed at the couch in the picture and said, "I like this charcoal color and modern style. I think it'd fit well with the overall theme we're going for. I don't like the lamps, though."

Autumn stepped next to the woman, ringing her hands together as she offered a suggestion. "Well, we can get rid of them completely, or we can look for another style to fit the theme."

Mrs. Peterson shoved the illustration into Autumn's arm. She barely had time to grab it, but she managed the split-second maneuver. As Mrs. Peterson wandered around the sixteen by twenty-one–foot living room, Autumn motioned with a quick bob of her head for Levi to help her out. He gave her a short nod and walked over to the older woman. Whipping out his phone, he said, "Here are some lamps that may be more suitable for the living room."

She snatched his phone from his hand and swiped through several pictures. Her eyebrows furrowed together before she shook her head with disdain. "No . . . Ugh, these just won't do. I think we should scrap the idea of lamps in here. What do you think, Luke?"

"What's that, dear?" Mr. Peterson asked as he looked up from running his hand over the marble countertop.

"The lamps, darling. In the living room. Yes or no?"

"I, uh . . . Well, whatever makes you happy."

Mrs. Peterson rolled her eyes and said to the two designers, "No lamps. We'll see how it looks once we get everything in here."

Autumn managed a tight smile and said, "We can do that. Is there anything else you'd like to change?"

She flicked her wrist dismissively. "Not at the moment. Let's go over the rest of the house before it gets too late."

♥♥♥♥♥♥

Autumn huffed as the Petersons finally stepped out of the home. It took almost two hours to walk through the whole house and figure out how the final designs should look. She loved being an interior decorator, but clients like the Petersons, made her want to rip her hair out. She leaned against the marbled kitchen counter and said, "Is it just me, or is Vivian Peterson the worst client we've had?"

Levi chuckled, adjusting his salmon-colored tie as he joined her at the counter. "She is definitely up there. I think Mrs. Fiera was the worst, though. If I recall, she hated every design we gave her and had us redo every room half-way through the decorating process."

"Ugh . . . yes. She also had that nasally voice and was super dramatic about everything."

"Yep, I'd say she's number one, but Vivian is definitely a close second."

Autumn turned to look at Levi. He'd been her friend for almost seventeen years, and he'd barely aged since their high school days. His fair skin was still wrinkle free, his jet-black hair smoothed back with gel, and his hazel eyes vibrant as always—a far cry from her own brown almond-shaped eyes. The only thing that had changed was his height as he'd grown from four foot seven to five foot ten. She had been mortified when he hit his growth spurt in tenth grade. Before that, she'd always stood an inch or two taller. Then, next thing you know, he sprouts a whole five inches over winter break. Autumn had hoped to catch up to him, or at least get closer in height, but she wound up staying a modest five foot four.

"Have any plans?" Levi asked, pulling her from her thoughts.

"No, not today. I'll probably just get some work done. How about you?"

"I have a date tonight with some guy I met on a dating app."

Autumn scrunched her eyebrows. "Wait . . . I thought you were dating Dylan?"

"We broke up a few weeks ago. I thought I told you."

Autumn wracked her brain but came up empty-handed. "I think I'd remember that."

Levi shrugged and said, "Well, we both wanted something different. He was ready to settle down, but I'm not quite at that stage of my life. So, we decided to part ways. He was super sweet, and I loved the guy, just not that way."

"I get it. A free spirit like you can't be tied down."

"You got that right. Not that I'd mind settling down, but there's still so much to do." He smiled down at her, nudging her playfully and asked, "How about you, little miss? You've been cooped up at work and locked away at home. You need to get out and live a bit."

Autumn scoffed. "I think you live enough for the both of us. Plus, I did just get this new haircut." She gestured to her short locks for emphasis.

"Oh yeah. . . Changing your haircut from mid-length to a pixie cut is really living life on the edge."

"Come on. You know how nervous I was to cut it to this length. It took me ten years, but I finally went through with it."

"I know." He patted her new 'do, running his fingers over her chocolate-brown hair. "It actually looks great on you. You should have done it sooner; it highlights your facial features and brings out your mahogany eyes."

She swatted his hand away with a small smirk before replacing it with a doubtful frown. She ran her own hand over her short cut and asked, "Do you really think it's okay?"

"Yes, I do. You're going to have all the men swarming around you during our next night out."

She gave him a cynical side glance. "Sure. Whatever you say."

"I'm giving you my honest opinion. I may be your best friend, but I wouldn't lie to you to make you feel good."

"Don't I know it. I'll never forget how you gave me a rough time when I was picking out my prom dress."

"I wanted to make sure you looked as fabulous as me."

Autumn giggled, craning her body to face him. "I actually just found our prom pictures in one of my bins. I should bring them over the next time we hang out."

"*Ooh*, yes. Let's go down memory lane." Levi tapped a finger against his chin for a couple of seconds. "How about this weekend? Mojitos and food that we'll regret eating by Monday."

"Sounds good to me."

Pushing off from the counter, they grabbed their belongings and exited the home, making sure to lock up before strolling down the walkway to the quiet street. Autumn tossed her briefcase and coat into the backseat, thankful that the rain had stopped, at least for now. Levi leaned against her open car door as she got into the driver's seat. She looked up at him with a smile. "See you at work tomorrow?"

"Maybe . . . Depending on what happens tonight," he answered with a mischievous wink.

"Well, good luck with your date. Don't do anything you'd usually do."

"You know I'm going to."

"I'm well aware, but since I said it, at least it's not on my conscience."

He chuckled and said, "You worry too much, Autumn. But I'll see you tomorrow, promise."

Levi shut her door before giving her a brisk wave as he headed to his own car. Autumn drove off, waving goodbye as she rolled past him. She was happy that he liked to put himself out into the world and embrace new experiences. She wished she could be more like him, but she always talked herself out of it. In the end, she was stuck being the laid-back and cautious friend. Though it *was* starting to take its toll. She hadn't gone on a date for at least three years now. Her last relationship ended in disastrous heartbreak, and she wasn't ready to go through that again. The truth was, she had no idea when, or even if, another guy would come along to make her want to love again.

Chapter 3

Elliot

Time ticked away slowly, but it was finally nearing the end of the day with just an hour to go. Only a few stray customers had drifted in and out throughout the workday. Most were locals, but there were a couple of out-of-towners who were just passing through. Right now, Elliot was helping Astrid clean up around the front counter, so they didn't have as much to do after closing. As he wiped down the countertop, a faint tap on the front window caught his attention. He glanced up to see his older sister enthusiastically waving at him. He rolled his eyes as he gave her a small wave back before motioning for her to come in. She sauntered through the front door with her golden-brown hair tied into a messy bun and her black pea-coat hugging her curves.

Astrid smiled brightly at Angela as she walked over to the counter. "I heard you were coming in. It's great to see you again, Angela."

"It's nice seeing you too. My brother hasn't been too tough on you, has he?" Angela asked, placing her hands on her hips with a playful smirk.

"He's a lamb. He can't even fire Matt, who's been late every single day."

"I'm not surprised. He's always been a bit of a pushover."

Elliot scoffed as he picked up a box of disposable napkins. "Oh, come on. I am not a pushover. I haven't fired Matt because it's the holiday season. Firing someone before Christmas would just be cruel."

Angela narrowed her eyes at him. "Okay, but what about the other three hundred and thirty days?"

He shook his head. "I don't have to explain myself to you."

"Sure, keep deflecting."

"I thought you came here for a friendly visit. Not to ridicule me."

Angela laughed as she eyed the front counter. She pointed to a few small plastic bags that were labeled: *Lawson's Thin Chip Cookies*. "*Those* are why I'm here."

Elliot picked up one of the bags from the wicker basket on the counter. He raised a brow at Angela and asked, "You're here for these disgusting cookies over your brother?"

"As much as I love you, I do love these little bite-size morsels even more. Besides, they've been in my life much longer than you have."

He rolled his eyes as he handed over the bag of cookies to his sister. She took them with a wide grin and unwrapped the bow that held them closed. Angela didn't waste any time popping one into her mouth, letting out a small groan of delight as she chewed.

"Is it to your satisfaction?" Elliot asked.

Still munching on her cookie, she mumbled, "Mhmm . . . Even better than I remember."

Elliot turned to Astrid and asked, "Can you close up tonight?"

She nodded. "Of course. You two have fun."

He said his thanks before heading off to the back to grab his things. It didn't take him long, and before he knew it, he and his sister were strolling down the sidewalk of their hometown as flurries spiraled down from the skies. Angela continued to snack on her cookies as she looked around at the evergreen garlands, colorful lights, and gold-dusted angel decorations adorning the lamp posts. She let out a blissful sigh and said, "It's always so beautiful this time of year."

"Only because you're here for so little time," Elliot said.

"Just because I'm not here all December long, doesn't mean I can't admire its beauty."

"Yes, but I see these over-decorated streets every day, and every year. The holiday season is just annoying these days."

"You're just a scrooge." She popped another cookie into her mouth and then asked, "What are you doing for Christmas, anyway?"

He looked at her, confused, and said, "I don't know. I thought we would spend it together this year."

"You know I go to Paris every year."

"Come on, Angela. We haven't had a Christmas together in years."

"We've had many wonderful Christmases together."

Elliot gave her a stern look. "I was four when you went to Paris for the first time."

She shrugged and said with a slight chuckle, "Okay. So, we had three wonderful Christmases together, even if you can't remember them."

He sighed while they continued to meander down the sidewalk, a brisk wind caressing their faces as the snowfall began to lighten. "I was just hoping for something different. Christmas has been hard since our parents passed. It gets kind of lonely this time of year."

Angela's smile fell. "I know, Elliot. If I hadn't already made plans, I'd stay here to celebrate with you."

He forced a tight smile. "It's fine. I'll figure something out, just like I do every year."

"Why don't you find yourself a date or start a hobby? That could keep you occupied."

Elliot shook his head and replied, "I'm too busy to have a hobby. I have to keep dad's business afloat."

Angela rolled her eyes. "I'm sure one day off work won't kill the café."

Elliot thought for a moment. "I don't even know what I'd do. There's not much going on around here."

"You used to love painting. I'm sure the rec' center still has painting classes at night."

"I'm not really into painting anymore. And it's not like I can make a career out of it."

"I, for one, think it would be good for you to meet some

new people and have a little fun." A silence hung between the two for a few seconds before Angela spoke again. "Well, if you don't want to do that, how about finding that date?"

"I'm not looking for anyone right now," he stated. "Plus, you haven't settled down with anyone yet. Why do I *need* to?"

"I didn't say anything about settling down. Just . . . find someone to spend time with."

"I guess I could find a friend to hang out with."

Her eyes lit up. "That too. I have tons of awesome girlfriends in New York. We go out every weekend for drinks or a movie. A couple of them are even coming to Paris."

They stopped walking and sat down on a bench in the tree-studded local park skirting the edge of town. The snow had stopped falling, but the air was still dreary and cold, especially since the sun was setting. Elliot crossed his arms in front of his chest in an attempt to stay warm and said, "I guess a friend couldn't hurt. I haven't gotten out much since I took over the café."

"That's the spirit," Angela said as she pulled him into a tight side hug. "I want to hear about all the crazy adventures you get into with your future friend."

"It's Shadow Birch, not Miami. Any adventures will be pretty boring."

"With that attitude and lack of imagination, they will be. Back in high school and college, my buddies and I would sneak into the next town over and do the stupidest things."

Elliot shrugged one shoulder. "I mean, I used to sneak

out and grab a beer or two with my friends, but that was about it."

"You never had a wild side, Elliot. That's probably why Dad left the café to you, besides me being in New York."

Elliot mulled over that thought. "I guess I was just always trying to be smart about what I did."

"Which was great because it turned you into a responsible man. Maybe a little *too* responsible, but I'm sure you'll get your personal life back to a somewhat normal state."

Elliot stood from the bench, stretching his stiff legs and back. He turned to his sister, who had finally eaten the last of her cookies. "Why don't we head home, and I'll cook us some dinner?"

Angela hopped to her feat, beaming. "Sounds good to me. I haven't had a decent home-cooked meal in months."

They finished the last bites of the supper Elliot prepared, a pot of pasta pomodoro. After cleaning up, they hung out on his couch, watching some movie they happened to stumble across while channel surfing. Not that they were paying much attention. They were too busy catching each other up on what had been happening in their lives since the last time they'd hung out.

"How long are you here for again?" Elliot asked.

Angela wore a thoughtful expression as she took a sip of her red wine. "I think a few days. I don't want to rush back to New York, but there are still a couple of things I need to get done before I head to Paris."

"I guess that's not too bad. I wish we could spend more time together, but I'll take what I can get."

She gave him an apologetic look. "I wish that too, but I need to put in a few more hours at work. Paris isn't paying for itself."

Elliot nodded as he picked up his bottle of beer from the coffee table and took a swig. "I guess it wouldn't. What are you planning to do while you're there?"

She shrugged as she tapped her index finger on the wine glass dangling from her hand. "Not sure. I promised my friends we'd visit the Eiffel Tower since they've never been before. I may go to a show or two with Remy."

"Remy? Who's he?"

"I thought I told you about him. We met during my third trip to Paris. We hang out together every year, and he shows me around. As a local, he knows all the best spots."

Elliot raised an eyebrow at his sister. "Are you two together?"

Angela scoffed before taking another sip of wine. "No, we're just friends. He lives in France, and I live in New York. It would never work out."

"All right, I was just curious. Since you spent a little over twenty years hanging out with him every December, I just assumed there was something more going on."

"I mean, he's sweet and only a couple of years older than me, but the distance would be tough to manage."

"That's understandable." Elliot downed the last of his beer before he spoke again. "You know, you keep talking about my love life. How about yours?"

"There's nothing to talk about," she explained,

shrugging her right shoulder as she cocked her head. "I've been with a few guys here and there, but none of them were happy with my work schedule. Plus, they all wanted a family."

Elliot stared back at his sister, wondering why this subject never came up before. "You don't want a family?"

"I don't know. It was never something I was keen on pursuing."

Elliot pondered her answer. "Never been my plan either. Actually, I never really had any sort of plan for when I got older, but it certainly wouldn't have looked like where I am now."

"I guess we never know where life is going to take us." She downed the rest of her drink. "But I think we're doing a great job so far."

He nodded half-heartedly as he stood with his empty beer bottle, trying to push down the feelings of mediocrity that threatened to dampen his mood. He reached a hand out toward his sister's empty glass and asked, "Would you like a refill?"

After handing it over to him, she put her index and thumb close together. "Just a smidge if you can. I have a brunch date with a few friends from high school tomorrow, and I don't want to feel like crap."

As Elliot made his way to the kitchen, he said over his shoulder, "Wine makes you feel that way?"

"Once you get older, you'll know the feeling. It just doesn't sit the same."

"Well, I guess I have about a decade and a half left before I learn how that feels," he said as he grabbed a cold beer bottle from the fridge and carefully refilled Angela's glass from the wine bottle on the counter.

"Ugh, don't remind me that I'm *that* much older than you." She let out a dramatic sigh and continued, "When you're my age, I'll be around the age our parents were just before they . . ."

Elliot came back with their drinks, handing the quarter glass of wine to Angela. As he sank into the plush couch next to her, taking a sip from his new beer, he said, "I don't want to think about it. About them."

A silence cloaked the room as they drank their beverages. Finally, Angela decided to change the subject, gesturing to something across the room. "You kept that old thing?"

Elliot glanced at the cherry-red rotary phone perched on an antique wooden table. It stood right below the main window in the living room, and he could vaguely see snowflakes floating down outside against the dark sky. "I did. I tried to keep most of the stuff we grew up with."

"You're so sentimental, I don't know why a woman hasn't scooped you up yet," Angela joked as she pinched Elliot's left cheek.

He pushed her hand away with a huff. "It was our great grandmother's, and I haven't had the heart to throw it out. Not to mention the time. Plus, I checked to see how much it would cost to upgrade this place into a bachelor pad, and let's just say it's a little out of my budget range."

"Does it even work?" she asked, referring to the phone.

"It does. Usually only telemarketers call, but Aunt Jane and Uncle Don have rung in a few times on special occasions."

"They must be in their eighties now, right?"

"Yeah, and it shows every time they call the rotary,"

Elliot said with a chuckle.

Angela let out her own snicker and said, "They've acted like they were in their eighties well before they hit that age. I remember Thanksgiving dinner when you were ten, and Aunt Jane lost her hearing aid in the mashed potato bowl."

"I remember that. We spent hours listening to her yell out questions, and us having to yell our answers back."

"Yep, until little cousin Mikey wound up spitting out the aid onto his plate of food."

Elliot grimaced at the memory. "Ugh, the thought of having that mixed in our food."

Angela nodded as she squirmed in her seat. "So gross."

They continued to laugh and joke about their family memories until late into the evening. Once they finished their drinks, they called it a night and headed off to bed. Elliot wasn't sure exactly why, but it was the lightest he'd felt in a long time.

Chapter 4

Autumn

Christmas was a week away, and Autumn was hunkered down in her office, sketching a layout design for a new client. She was just putting some finishing touches on the master bedroom when a light knock sounded on her half-open door. Before she could address the visitor, her boss waltzed in, skimming through an interior design magazine. Autumn straightened up. "May I help you, Mrs. Lamour?"

Mrs. Lamour slid her thin black glasses down the bridge of her nose, staring at Autumn over the rims. "I want you to look through this magazine. I'm hoping we can incorporate some of these new trends into the Hughes' home."

"I thought we weren't going to start on their home until after New Year's."

"A slight change of plans. We're moving all our other clients to after the new year, and the Hughes' home should be completed a few days before New Year's Eve."

Autumn twirled her pencil in her hand, feeling uneasy. "That doesn't give us much time, ma'am."

"We have plenty of time if we do it right." She slapped the magazine down on Autumn's desk with a petite hand that was starting to wrinkle with age. "You're my best designer as of now. I know you can do this, and that you won't let me down. At least, you better not."

Autumn rushed out an answer. "I'll try my best, but I can't do it alone."

"I already thought about that, and your partner should be here soon to chat with you."

Autumn cocked her head, wondering who her boss may have set her up with. She almost always worked with Levi, but since this was a tougher project, maybe Mrs. Lamour wanted a more experienced hand in it. "Who is my partner?"

Her boss clasped her hands together, a small grin playing on her dark-pink lips. "Rodney. You two worked so well together on the Deller house a couple of years ago, I wanted you two to collaborate again."

"Oh, your son . . ." She gritted her teeth and mumbled under her breath, *"That's just great."*

"Yes, that's right. You two both do a swell job here, so I can't wait to see what you come up with." She started sashaying toward the door and called over her shoulder, "Good luck, Autumn."

With that, she was gone, leaving Autumn to dwell on the fact that she'd be working with her boss's son again. The pompous jerk had an annoying crush on her. It wasn't even a real crush—he just never had a woman turn him down, and it clearly irked him that she couldn't be another notch in his belt. If he wasn't so arrogant, she'd probably give him a chance. After all, he was good at his job and decent looking. But his attitude was enough to turn her off.

As these thoughts crossed her mind, the man himself waltzed through her office door with a wry smirk on his delicate lips. He strutted over toward Autumn's desk like he owned the place—which he practically did, since his mother was the boss. He dropped down into the seat across her desk, running a hand through his wavy golden-bronze hair that he always kept trimmed to a decent length. He leaned back with ease as his hand found the light stubble on his face. "Looking good, beautiful."

"Drop dead, Rodney," she retorted with narrowed eyes.

Rodney held both arms out to his sides with his palms up as he let out a short scoff. "What? Can't I compliment my favorite work partner?"

"No, because that's called sexual harassment. Maybe you should look into it, or perhaps I can ask HR to do it for you."

"Listen, Autumn. I know you dislike me for whatever reason, but if you just gave me a chance, you'd see I'm actually a pretty cool guy."

She crossed her arms in front of her chest and said, "Okay then. If you promise to behave and work on this project in a civilized manner, I'll try to conceal my blatant distaste for you."

"Sounds good to me." Rodney stood up and added, "I'm going to work on some plans for the Hughes' home, and you should do the same. We'll swap notes tomorrow and figure out a strategy. Maybe we'll swing over to the house on Wednesday for a look-through to brainstorm more ideas."

"Fine, we'll do that."

He gave her a charming smile before sauntering toward the door. "See you tomorrow, Autumn."

He left her door open, which annoyed her, but within seconds, Levi walked through the door. He shut it behind him as he meandered toward the seat Rodney had just occupied. Hitching a thumb back at the door, he asked, "What was he doing here?"

"Mrs. Lamour wants me to work on the Hughes house with him," Autumn answered with a sigh.

"Ugh, seriously? You got stuck with him again?" He flopped into the seat and shook his head. "He's such a jerk. I can barely handle five minutes with the guy."

"Believe me, if I had a say in it, I'd be working with you, or any of our other colleagues, for that matter."

"Oh, I know. If you said anything about her darling boy, she'd have you packing up in a heartbeat."

"Yeah, remember David?"

"No . . ." A smirk sprang to his lips as he said, "Kidding. I do. He was barely here a month before she kicked him out. I forget what happened, though."

"From what Mrs. Lamour said, he had the audacity to tell her boy that he was an egotistical rat who stole his ideas, and those of many others at the office, passing them off as his own to make his mommy proud."

"I mean, he wasn't wrong. He's stolen a few of our ideas since we started working here."

Autumn nodded. "Yeah, like the last project Rodney and I worked on. I came up with most of the ideas. Like the open space in the foyer, which the Dellers loved. He stole all the glory from that design."

Levi grimaced and said, "I wish we could put him in his place, but I guess that'll never happen assuming we want to keep our jobs."

"Yeah, taking him down a peg sure would be nice."

Levi stood from his seat and said, "Maybe there'll be a day when karma comes for Mr. Mama's Boy."

"It can't come soon enough," Autumn said with a chuckle.

As he waltzed toward the door, Levi said, "Well, I'll let you get to your work. I'm sure the faster you get done with the Hughes' house, the better."

She sank deeper into her chair with a resigned sigh. "Yep."

He left, closing the door behind him just like Autumn preferred. And just like that, she was alone with her thoughts once again. Figuring she should start getting ideas for the Hughes home, she picked up the magazine Mrs. Lamour had dropped off and started jotting information down.

Wednesday arrived before Autumn knew it, and she was eagerly waiting outside of the Hughes home. She had been standing there for about an hour, hoping Rodney would arrive soon. It was another frigid day in Seattle, so she was bundled accordingly in a heavy coat, long jeans, gloves, and boots. Even though she was dressed for the weather, the bitter wind still chilled her to the bones. She would have gone inside if she had the key, but no. Rodney was the only person who carried them. She pulled out her phone to call the man, but before she could, his sleek black Lamborghini pulled into the driveway. Rodney stepped out of his car with swagger and fixed the collar of his beige suede coat. He was both impeccably dressed and well-guarded against the cold.

Autumn crossed her arms and let out a huff. "You were supposed to be here an hour ago."

Rodney pulled his sleeve back to reveal a silver watch on his lightly tanned arm. His brows drew together, and he exhaled a quick puff of vapor as he looked at the time. "I didn't realize it was that late. I had a lady friend over last night and—you know . . ."

Autumn waved off his excuse. "I don't want to know. I just want to get this over with."

"Suit yourself."

He opened the front door, and they entered the empty home that stood like a blank canvas. Autumn didn't waste time as she took in the wooden floors, white walls, and limited space in each section of the home. She whipped out the notebook she carried to every design project and jotted down new plans to run against the ideas they'd come up with on Tuesday.

"What're you doing over the holiday?" Rodney asked.

"What?" Autumn wasn't really listening as she was too

busy thinking up living room concepts.

"Christmas. Do you have any plans?"

The question brought a pang to her chest. Her mother didn't live close by, and now that her sister had moved, she'd be alone this Christmas. Mustering up a casual tone, she answered, "Not anything in particular. Why?"

Rodney shrugged nonchalantly as his hands slipped into his coat pockets. "I was just wondering. We have our meeting with the Hughes on Friday, and I know we usually have off on the weekend, especially since Christmas falls on Monday this year."

"Are you asking me to work during the holiday?" Autumn inquired with a frown. Would he really be that thoughtless?

"Not at all. Only the weekend."

She released a long breath through her nose, thinking it over. "Well, I guess I don't mind."

"Great." Rodney leaned against the empty wall. "We'll run our ideas by them on Friday, figure out what they're looking for design-wise, and acquire some of the products while polishing our plans over the weekend."

"That's fine, as long as we can get this done by next Friday. Even if we have to work overtime."

"I'm glad you see it that way."

Autumn scribbled down more notes and took a few snapshots with her phone to remember where some of the permanent fixtures were located. They already had blueprints and a digital layout of the home, but she liked using personal photographs to help her better visualize her design concepts. She cocked her head, studying the walls. "Don't you think a navy-blue paint would fit the aesthetic better?"

"If the Hughes like it, sure. I still think ecru is more fitting."

"We'll run both by them. Or they can choose a color from one of our palettes."

Rodney followed Autumn from room to room, barely putting his two cents in unless she asked him for input. His lack of participation was grinding on her nerves, but at least he wasn't running his mouth like usual. As they finished up, Rodney finally decided to talk, but not about the project as she hoped. "So, you're not doing anything for Christmas, right?"

"No, Rodney. Why does it matter?" Autumn folded her arms defensively and jutted her hip to the side.

"I have no plans either. My mother is heading to Fiji with her new boyfriend Ken, so I'll be alone too."

"Why don't you go out with one of the many bimbos you've snagged over the years? I'm sure they'll swarm to you in a heartbeat."

"I could, but I'd rather extend an invitation to you."

Autumn couldn't believe the nerve of this guy. "Well, I decline."

"You don't even know what I had in mind."

Autumn gritted her teeth, strutting out the front door with haste. Rodney trailed behind her as she said, "I don't want to hang out with you."

"Not even in Tokyo? I know a great place for sushi," he mentioned as he continued following her.

She spun on her heel once she reached her car and said, "Listen, Rodney. You can't woo me with your fancy stuff and spontaneous trips out of the country. It's not going to work."

He scowled. "Why are you playing so hard to get?"

"I'm not. I don't like you, end of story. All I want to do is finish this project so we can go our separate ways, until your mother pairs us up for another assignment."

Rodney pressed his lips together as he cocked his head to the side. "You'll come around. I mean, you can't resist me forever."

"I can and I will," Autumn boomed as she slid into her vehicle. "Now if you'll excuse me, I have some information to write up before Friday's meeting. Have a good afternoon."

As she took off down the road, red-hot anger burned her ears. Rodney was getting on her last nerve as he continued to pursue her, even though she'd told him her true feelings a dozen times. Either his thick skull couldn't comprehend her rejections, or he simply chose not to. All she wanted was to make it to Christmas so she could unwind with some eggnog and classic Christmas movies. Hopefully, that would help her get through the rest of the week until the project was wrapped up. Then she could relax once more with a bottle of champagne on New Year's Eve.

And amid all that, she'd have to remember to give her sister a call to wish her happy holidays. She probably didn't have many friends yet in Vermont, so Autumn was sure the gesture would mean a lot to her.

Chapter 5

Elliot

Festive music filled the air as a black-and-white Christmas flick played on the television. Elliot was nursing his second glass of eggnog as he lounged on his couch, zoning in and out of the movie. This was what his typical Christmas looked like these days, he realized. A kind of tradition, some may say. He was waiting for his sister to phone him to wish him a merry Christmas, just like she always did. Since it was going on three in the afternoon in Vermont, it would be about nine at night in Paris. He usually hated calling his sister owing to the time difference. He'd rather her call him, so he didn't wind up bothering her.

He started rising from his sofa to pour himself another glass of eggnog when the rotary phone's shrill ring echoed through the room. He rolled his eyes, figuring that his aunt and uncle were calling to wish him well during the holiday. Elliot answered the phone without hesitation. "Hello, this is Elliot."

"Oh, jeez . . . I'm so sorry," a female voice he didn't recognize fumbled on the other end. "I must have misdialed."

"It's fine. I've done it too."

"My sister just moved to Vermont, so I thought I'd call her." She sighed and mumbled, "Not that you care about my life story. Sorry to bother you."

Elliot surprised himself, as well as the random caller, when he blurted out, "Wait . . ."

"Um . . . what?"

He stuttered as he tried to figure out what to say next. Where had that come from? Maybe he was just a little too buzzed from the heavy booze in his eggnog, but part of him wanted to chat with this unknown woman. "I know this will sound really weird, but I wouldn't mind chatting for a while. I mean, if you want."

"You want to talk to me? A complete stranger?" the woman asked over the phone, her tone skeptical.

"I know . . . it's ridiculous. I guess it's just the eggnog making decisions for me."

"Oh, yeah. It does that to me too. Thankfully, I haven't tapped into my stash yet."

Elliot twisted the cord of the cherry-red rotary phone around his finger. "How come?"

"It's only noon, and I like to get my holiday calls out of

the way before I check out for the rest of the day."

"I know how that goes," Elliot said as he breathed out a short chuckle. "So, you live in California?" He threw out the random guess, hoping he'd nail it on the first try.

"No, Washington state."

"Ah, nice. I have a few relatives there."

"It's a decent place if you don't mind the rain."

Elliot sat down on his couch as he adjusted the bulky phone in his hand. He ran a hand over his face and said, "Man, I never thought I'd see the day when I'd chat with a stranger on the phone. I remember when my grandpa used to spend hours on the phone with random telemarketers because he wanted someone to talk to."

"My grandmother used to do that with cashiers. I hated when we'd hold up the line so she could tell the clerk what her cat did that day," the woman said with a sweet laugh. "By the way, my name is Autumn."

"I'm Elliot."

"It's nice to meet you."

"You too."

"So, you don't have any family in the area?" Autumn asked.

Elliot shook his head, even though she couldn't see him, "No. My sister lives in New York, but she visits Paris every Christmas, so that's where she is now. Most of my other close relatives are scattered across the country."

"Your parents?"

"They're both . . ." —he cleared his throat— "They're gone."

"I'm sorry to hear that. My father passed away when I was eleven."

"Thanks. I'm sorry about your father."

"Thank you."

Elliot propped his feet up on the walnut coffee table in front of his couch and asked, "How about you? Any family or friends near you?"

Autumn breathed a short hum before she answered him. "Not really, no. Like I mentioned, my sister just moved to Vermont. Her husband got a job over there, and they thought it was too good of an opportunity to pass up. My mother moved to Florida a few years ago with my stepdad. And my closest friend is visiting his own family."

"Huh. Well, what's that say about us? Everyone else is uprooting their lives and moving on. Yet we're stuck in the same place."

"Well, I don't know about you, but I have a wonderful job that'll help open doors for me if I stay long enough."

"My job is keeping me where I am too. Albeit it's not as glamorous as yours sounds. It's my dad's coffee shop that I inherited when he passed. Most of my time is spent making sure Lawson's Bistro stays afloat."

"Wow, that doesn't sound too bad to me."

"It is when a whopping majority of customers are the people you've known your whole life. We only get a few random out-of-towners every once in a while, so it gets kind of monotonous."

"Yeah, I guess that would take the fun out of owning a business." She let out a sigh and added, "To tell you the truth, my job isn't as great as I make it out to be. Sure, it can help me get my foot in the door with other agencies, but my boss is a stern woman, and her son is a snobbish pig who won't take no for an answer."

"What do you do, anyway?" he asked, sipping his creamy eggnog that coated his tongue with a sharp hint of nutmeg.

"I'm an interior decorator."

Elliot perked up and said, "A decorator? I could use one of those. I've been trying to fix my parents' home up to make it fit my style, but I've been struggling with ideas. It's not cheap, either."

"Prices have been pretty steep lately for certain furniture items and paint. Hopefully, the costs will come down soon."

"So, I should wait a bit longer?"

"Yeah, at least a year, maybe two. The prices should start to settle."

Elliot chuckled and said, "That's good to know. If I take anything from this random phone call, it's when to start my home decorating project."

"I'm glad I could help."

They both laughed heartily, and Elliot wound up chatting for hours with Autumn. They talked about their lives, their jobs, and everything in between. He felt like he could open up and be himself with her, which made him wish she didn't live over two thousand miles away. Their phone call was finally interrupted when Elliot's cellphone rang. He checked the caller ID, seeing that his sister was trying to reach him. He let out a short sigh. He didn't want this unusual phone call to end, but he couldn't ignore his sister.

"I enjoyed talking to you Autumn, but I have to take this call," Elliot explained into the antique receiver.

"It's not a problem," she said as Elliot heard shuffling,

making the phone crackle a bit. "Wow, I didn't realize we were on for three hours. I guess I should finish my Christmas calls as well. It was nice talking to you, Elliot."

"Hey, if neither of us have any plans next Christmas, would you like to chat again?"

"You know what, why not? We'll make it our last resort if we find ourselves alone during the holiday once more."

"Hearing it that way makes it sound much more depressing."

"It does. Well, maybe we'll have plans next year. We could still give each other a call, though."

"Sounds good. I'd like that," Elliot said, smiling to himself. "Goodbye, Autumn."

"Bye, Elliot," her gentle voice echoed from across the continent.

And just like that, they hung up. Elliot quickly clicked the green answer button on his more modern smartphone before it could go to voicemail. He greeted Angela with a short, "Hello."

"I was beginning to think you'd never answer. You didn't overdo it with the eggnog again, did you?" His big sister snickered on the other end.

"No. I've only had two glasses."

"That's good to hear. So, how's your Christmas going?"

He sank back into the couch. "It'd be better with someone to spend it with, but I did have a great conversation with someone over the phone."

"This person's real, right? You're not cracking up on me?"

"She's real," he answered with a grumble. "Her name is Autumn, and she lives in Seattle."

"Seattle . . .? What are you doing talking to someone out there?"

He explained how the whole phone call came about, gushing over all the details that made their conversation special. Once he was done, all he heard on the other end was Angela cackling in the background. He let out a small burst of air through his nose and said, "It's not that funny."

"Oh, but it is . . ." He heard her breathing heavily as she tried to control her fit of laughter. "You went full Grandpa Lou on her."

He couldn't help but smirk. "I guess I did."

"Did you at least ask her to meet you at the top of the Empire State Building on Valentine's Day?"

Elliot scoffed and said, "Come on. This isn't *Sleepless in Seattle*."

"You're right. It's vastly different. He lived in Seattle with his son, while she lived in Baltimore with her fiancé. Still would have been cute, though."

He sighed. "Can we drop this?"

"All right." Angela changed the subject and said, "Well, my Christmas was quite eventful. The girls and I went to a special Christmas event at the Louvre. They had some beautiful decorations, and a few local artists displayed their holiday-themed paintings."

"Gee, sounds grand," Elliot said, unable to hide a hint of jealousy.

"Don't act like I'm leaving you out. I've invited you several times since college, but you always declined."

"I know. I honestly wish I would have taken you up on those offers—instead of being cooped up in my childhood home every year, watching the same movies and listening to the same gleeful songs."

"And talking to strangers on the phone."

He threw his head back. "Ugh, can we not?"

"Oh, I'm just teasing you. But at least you had a somewhat eventful Christmas."

"Yeah, it wasn't too bad this year."

His sister sighed and said, "Hey, it's getting late over here. I just wanted to wish you a merry Christmas.

"Merry Christmas to you as well."

"Maybe next year you can come to Paris with me."

"Or you could stay here," Elliot ventured, trying to reason with her.

"We'll see."

They said their goodbyes, and he hung up the phone, placing it on his coffee table. He reclined back in his usual, well-worn spot on the couch and wondered what next Christmas would bring. He was actually looking forward to it, which was rare these days. Part of him would love to go to Paris with Angela, but the other part was hoping that Autumn would call him again, just like they planned. Of course, he couldn't rely on a what-if scenario. Anything could happen in the next 365 days. Elliot figured he'd just take things day by day during the new year and came to a decision before the holidays come around once again.

Chapter 6

Autumn

Autumn felt lighter than air as she bounced toward her office the day after Christmas. As she set her things down and organized her desk, Levi strolled through her door with confusion written on his face.

"You seem joyful this morning. Which is not like you at all." Levi crossed his arms over his chest. "Spill it, sister."

"I had a good holiday. That's it," she said with a smirk tugging at her lips.

"Is that so? As I recall, you were disappointed last week because your mom and sister weren't here to celebrate. Then, to top it all off, Mrs. Lamour put you on an assignment, which made you miss our trip to Oregon to visit my family."

"I didn't celebrate Christmas under the best circumstances, no. I was a smidge lonely, but guess what? When I tried to call my sister, I made a small error when inputting the number."

"You dialed the wrong number? How'd that change your holiday from terrible to amazing?"

"It was weird," Autumn said as she recalled her Christmas conversation with a complete stranger. "I was keen on hanging up and redialing Jillian's number. But the man I called, Elliot, asked if I wanted to chat since we were both alone for the holiday."

Levi raised a mischievous eyebrow as he gave her an open-mouthed grin. He took a seat in the chair across of her desk, leaning in with his right elbow on his leg and chin cradled in the palm of his hand. "This man has a name? Do tell me more."

Autumn shrugged as she tried to cover the smile that was creeping over her face. "There's not much to tell. We talked for a few hours about our lives, everything from work to some personal things. It was nice."

"You had an hours-long conversation with the man, and all you can tell me is that it was nice. I mean, is he hot? Is he single? Where does he live?"

"I don't know. I never saw him, and all I know is that he lives somewhere in Vermont. Though the way he talked, I didn't get the impression he was dating anyone, or wasn't in a serious relationship, anyway."

"Hmm . . . Interesting."

"What's so interesting?" Rodney asked as he strutted into the room, dressed smartly in his sleek black suit and dark-blue tie.

"Nothing that concerns you, Rodney," Levi said as he got up from the seat.

"Is that so, Davidson? And don't you have work to do?

"Yes. I was just leaving."

Levi moved to leave the room, but not before casting Autumn a sympathetic look. Autumn returned her friend's gaze briefly before eyeing the man who decided to lean against her desk. As he thumbed through the papers on her desktop, not even sparing her a glance, he asked, "Did you have a good holiday?"

She was already annoyed with the guy, and it was only nine in the morning. She wasn't quite sure how she was going to manage working with him for the rest of the day—and the next few days after. In a brisk motion, Autumn snatched the papers Rodney was rifling through and stuffed them in one of her drawers. She looked up at Rodney, who was giving her a cheeky smirk, and answered, "It was fine."

"Mine too. I decided to head to Japan anyway with a couple of models that I'd met during my time in Milan. The ladies and I had a wonderful time, though I do wish you'd been with me instead."

"That'll never happen." She crossed her arms in front of her and said, "Now, can we get down to business and finish the Hughes' home?"

"Sure. We have another meeting with them in a couple of hours at their house. We should have most of our design ideas prepared by then."

"Then let's get to it."

As she worked alongside Rodney, her mind couldn't stop wandering to the man she'd talked to on the phone.

Elliot seemed like a nice guy based on their conversation, and as crazy as it sounded, she couldn't wait for next Christmas to come around so she could speak to him again.

Chapter 7

Elliot

Elliot couldn't stop himself from whistling a merry Christmas tune as he set up the shop for opening. As he pulled out a fresh bag of espresso beans, he realized he hadn't felt this chipper in years. He would have never thought a phone call with a stranger would make him feel this way. As he turned on the coffee and espresso machines, Astrid waltzed into the seating area while putting her hair in a bun. She slipped behind the counter and looked at Elliot skeptically.

"You're smiling . . . What's going on?" she asked him, blunt as always.

Elliot let out a snort of laughter. "What do you mean? I always smile."

"No, not like this. This is like a pure, genuine smile. I haven't seen you like this since, well, you know . . ."

"Maybe I'm just trying to turn things around. Can't get anywhere in life by thinking negative all the time."

"I guess you're right," Astrid said as she got the cash register ready for the day. "I just hope it stays, because it looks good on you, Elliot."

"I'm going to do my best," he said, shooting her a quick smirk.

"But what's the main reason for this sudden change?"

"Does there have to be a reason?"

She thought for a moment. "Yeah . . . No one wakes up one morning and says they're going to flip their mood around just out of the blue."

"If you really want to know, I talked to a woman from across the country yesterday, and it made me reflect on my life after we hung up."

Astrid cocked her head. "Odd. Did you know her?"

He explained the whole, bizarre Christmas-day scenario to Astrid. When he finished, she looked at him like he had just told her he'd been on the phone with the Ghost of Christmas Present. "You roped a stranger into talking to you for three hours? If I was her, I totally would have hung up on you as soon as I realized I had the wrong number."

He nodded and said, "I thought she'd do that, but she seemed receptive when I asked her if she wanted to talk. She was sweet, and she kept the conversation rolling better than I would have imagined."

Astrid had a sparkle in her eye as she said, "At least you had a great Christmas. I know it's been a while since you had one."

"Thanks."

"Think she'll call you next year?"

"It would be nice, but who knows where life will take us by then?"

"That's true. Well, whatever may happen, I hope this new side of you stays and leads you to find a new life of happiness."

He gave her a tight nod before stepping into the back. Matt and Andrew strolled through the backdoor of the shop. As they hung up their coats and scarves, Elliot said to them, "Glad to see you guys. And Matt, thanks for getting here on time."

"I'm trying my best. Now that college classes are out for winter break, I can go to sleep earlier than usual," Matt said.

Elliot furrowed his brow. "I didn't know you were still taking courses."

"Yeah, but only a couple here and there. I was going to quit, but I thought I'd stick with it since I'm almost done."

Elliot looked at his young employee with new eyes. "Well, good for you. If you ever need some time off, don't hesitate to let me know."

Matt cocked his head to the side and looked at Elliot, his eyebrows scrunching together. "You are on the verge of firing me, aren't you?"

Elliot shook his head with a grimace. "No, I'm not going to fire you."

"You just seem way too nice today. Not that you're not nice all the time, but this seems different."

Andrew nodded as he chimed in, "I have to agree with Matt here. You do seem different, like a weight has been lifted off your shoulders."

Astrid walked into the room and said, "He chatted with a woman who had the wrong number, and now he's smitten."

Andrew's face lit up. "Oh, so you're looking to get back out there? Good for you, my friend."

Elliot shrugged and answered, "Not really. It just kind of put my life in perspective."

Matt patted his boss's shoulder and said, "Hey, whatever gets you out of that brooding mood you're sulking through half the time. By the way, is she hot, and does she have a friend?"

Elliot narrowed his eyes at the younger man and said, "Why don't you start setting up the tables?"

"I got it . . . I got it . . ." Matt mumbled as he shuffled to the front of the café.

Andrew gripped Elliot's left shoulder and said, "I am happy for you, El. That phone call does seem like it sparked something in you."

Elliot put on a half-smile and said, "It made me realize that I need some balance in my life. My sister tried telling me the same thing while she was here, but I guess it didn't register until I started making conversation with a stranger over the telephone. Anyway, I do think some friends, a hobby, or even a relationship may be good for me."

"If you ever want to hang out with Paul and me, along with the kids, don't hesitate to drop by. We'd love some extra competition on game nights."

"I'll make sure to drop by sometime. I can't pass up a game night."

The man smiled at him before hitching a thumb to the kitchen. "I'm going to whip up a few Christmas cookies for the customers. I know they enjoy them this time of year."

"Sure thing."

As Andrew retreated to the kitchen, Elliot made his way back to the front of the café and found Sophia scuttling toward the front door. She tapped on the glass, waving her gloved hand at him anxiously from outside. He sighed as he dragged his feet over to the door, unlocking it to let her in.

"We're not open yet, Sophia," Elliot said.

"I'm aware of that. But I have a root canal in ten minutes, and I need my coffee."

"Can't you just make it at home?"

"Our coffee maker is broken. And let's be real, your shop's coffee is way better than my home brew."

"Fair point." Elliot hooked his thumbs in his pockets as he turned to Astrid behind the counter. "Can you get Sophia's order ready?"

Astrid nodded, grabbing a paper cup to start on Sophia's usual order. Sophia smiled wide before standing on her tiptoes to give Elliot a massive hug. She beamed up at him. "Thank you! You don't know how much this means to me."

He chuckled at her overdramatic enthusiasm. "I think I might."

Sophia cocked her head, squinting as she studied him. "Something's different about you . . ."

"What, I seem happier than normal?"

"I'm guessing others have noticed it too."

"Yep. Everyone has pointed it out." He looked down at his shoes, feeling his cheeks heating up. "I didn't think I was that bad."

She put a hand on his shoulder and said, "You know, you always had a happy-go-lucky attitude when we were kids. Then, when everything happened, you lost that spark, and I never thought you'd get it back."

"I guess us breaking up and my parents dying all around the same time, I did kind of shut down. Until now, I was just going through the motions."

"What brought about this sudden change?"

Elliot shrugged with an awkward grin. "I was having a boring Christmas as usual, and a woman called. We chatted for a while, and that was that."

A smirk crept onto his ex's lips, and she said, "Ooh . . . A woman. Is she nice? Is she from around here? Maybe you can take her as your plus-one to my wedding."

He held his palms up. "Calm down. We just met, and I don't even know what she looks like. She did seem nice, but it's too soon to ask her out on a date. Especially one involving my ex and her future husband."

"I guess you're right. When do you plan on meeting face to face?"

Elliot's shoulders slumped slightly as he felt a twinge of regret. "Probably never. She lives in Washington state."

Sophia's glowing smile slowly fell. "Ah, that's too bad. Maybe you two can meet someday."

He nodded. "You never know. For now, we promised to chat next Christmas if we have nothing planned, like this year."

"Well, whoever she is, I'm happy she was able to put a

smile on your face and change your perspective a bit."

"Me too," Elliot said, feeling the smallest spark of hope.

Astrid called from across the way, "Order's ready."

Sophia gave Elliot a quick smile before heading off to the counter to get her drink and muffin. Once she was done paying, she returned to Elliot with a wide grin. "Thanks again for letting me get this. And I hope that you grab that girl, because she seems good for you."

Elliot was dumbfounded. All he could say was, "Thank you."

Sophia said her goodbyes to everyone before hustling out of the café. Elliot turned to his employees and announced, "Let's get this workday started."

DECEMBER 2018

Chapter 8

Autumn

Levi was dancing off-beat to the Christmas music blaring from Autumn's cellphone. He grabbed a long, silver garland from one of the many decoration boxes that littered Autumn's floor, tossing the shiny tinsel around Autumn's waist and pulling her closer to him. He started shimmying and laughing as he continued to hop and sway to the festive tune. "Come on, Autumn. Dance with me."

She shook her head with a chuckle. "I think you're doing enough dancing for the both of us."

"Oh, come on. There's no one else here. Have a little fun."

"Well . . . okay, fine."

She rolled her eyes as she joined her friend in their

impromptu dance session. She grabbed one end of the garland and spun around, Levi following her lead. They shuffled over to her tree and started stringing it up as they continued to bop to the music.

Autumn adjusted one of the ornaments dangling off an artificial spruce branch and said, "I can't believe it's this time of year again. I feel like I just took my tree down."

"We did just take your tree down three months ago," Levi reminded her.

"I probably should have just left it up, if I'd known it'd be here in a blink of an eye."

"Nah, I like putting it back up. It gets me into the spirit."

"I thought that was the spiked eggnog."

"That does the trick too," Levi giggled as he hopped over to her kitchen counter, where the drink in question awaited. He took a sip from his rounded glass and asked, "Are you thinking about calling that guy?"

"What guy?" Autumn asked, confused.

"You know, the one you chatted with last Christmas."

Her eyes flew wide with the sudden recollection. "Oh, you mean Elliot. I'm not sure. He said if we didn't have any plans we could chat again, but I've made plans with you, so . . ."

"*So*, take an hour or two out of our schedule and call the dude. I won't be sticking around here all day."

"I don't know. He's probably busy." She sighed as she hung another ornament on the tree. "I mean, a lot can happen in a year. Like, I got a small career bump with that promotion, and since the work I did with Rodney, Mrs. Lamour has put me on tons of project assignments."

Levi grimaced. "Yeah, too bad you have to see more of

that egotistical jerk now that you're a big shot at the agency."

"It's not too bad. The meetings are brief, and I'm pretty sure he finally took a hint."

"There's no way he did. He's just planning something to woo your heart before he breaks it into a million little pieces like the playboy he is."

"Possibly. But for now, I'm happy with my position until something better comes along. *If* it comes along."

He nodded. "So, back to the mysterious stranger named Elliot. Why don't you give him a call? He might be just as eager to catch up as you are. You'll never know if you don't try."

Autumn hummed as she grabbed her glass of eggnog and took a sip of the ice-cold, creamy concoction with an aftertaste of smooth rum. "I guess I could give him a call. It's not like I have anything to lose, with him being over two thousand miles away."

Levi's face lit up. "Exactly! Go for it, girlie. You never know what may happen between the two of you."

"Not much, I presume. Long-distance relationships are tricky."

"True, most of them don't work out, but that doesn't mean they're one-hundred percent flawed." Levi took another swig from his glass and added, "You two can always meet in person sometime since your sister lives there."

"What difference would a face-to-face meetup make if we're still living thousands of miles apart?" Autumn asked, shrugging as a hint of melancholy pricked at her heart.

"Maybe when you finally catch a glimpse of him from across a crowded room, sparks will fly, and you'll fall head over heels. You always said you wanted that magical moment between you and your 'soulmate.' Maybe he's that guy."

She scoffed. "That's when I was twelve with braces and a bad haircut. I didn't know what I wanted, and I definitely had no clue what love was."

"Do you even know now?"

"No, but I'm sure I'll figure it out when I meet the right guy. I do know it's not going to be rainbows and butterflies when I finally find that special someone. And I'm also certain Elliot isn't him."

"All right." Levi nodded, seemingly accepting her answer—reluctantly. "I still say to give him a call and see where this leads. Sure, he may just be a nice guy to talk to while you're getting back on the dating horse, but it could be something more."

Autumn breathed out a resigned sigh. "I guess you have a point. I'll feel things out with him if we do chat again, but if nothing comes of it, I'll give up on it."

"That's all you can do." Levi picked up a box of loose silver tinsel and said, "Now, let's give this tree a little more pizazz."

"Ugh, I don't want to have to deal with those stringy, staticky foil strips. I'm always finding strands of them on my clothes or my furniture months after I've cleaned my holiday décor up."

His expression fell. "Oh, come on. Tinsel is the best part of tree decorating, and it makes everything sparkle."

"Fine, but if I find any leftover tinsel in any nook or

cranny of my apartment, I'm sending you a glitter bomb."

He smirked and said, "Don't threaten me with a good time, honey."

She chuckled, rolling her eyes as she mumbled, "Let's get this over with."

They returned to decorating, and Autumn soaked in their much-needed quality time together outside of work. As they finished their night with a *Miracle on 34th Street* double feature, Autumn's mind wandered to her upcoming call with Elliot. Maybe she had been too quick to shut down the idea of getting to know him and meeting him in person. After all, he could be the one for her. But which of them would sacrifice their livelihood to move across the country to be with the other? It certainly wasn't going to be her, especially since she was so close to achieving her dreams. And she doubted he'd take the plunge, even if he had grown weary of his hometown. They would be at an impasse—it would never work. By the end of the night, Autumn decided it'd be best if they remained friends and phone pals, no matter what happened during their next call.

Chapter 9

Elliot

"Put your back into it," Elliot grumbled as he watched his newest employee wipe down one of the café tables.

"Don't make me smack you with this rag," his sister retorted as she paused, wielding the soppy rag.

Elliot backed up with his hands raised in surrender as he said with a chuckle, "No need to be hostile."

Angela turned to him with a smirk. "If you keep bossing me around like this, there's no knowing what I'll do to you."

"Fair enough."

Her face softened as she leaned back against the table. "I wanted to thank you for giving me this job though."

"You're my sister, I'll do anything for you, whenever I

can. Plus, you took care of me when I was little, so I have to repay you somehow."

"Don't worry, Mom and Dad paid me plenty for my tiresome babysitting duties. But this café work is good too." Angela tossed the wet rag on the table as she placed her hands on her hips, studying the ceramic tiled floor. "I still can't believe they laid me off. Well, not just me, since a good majority of the people I worked with got canned, but still."

"I can't believe it either. To be honest, I'm always nervous there'll be a day I won't be able to pay the rent here, and I'll have to shut this place down. I'd hate to be the bearer of bad news to my workers if it happens, but it is my business."

Angela scrunched her nose in a scowl. "At least you care about your workers. Those big companies in New York didn't give a crap about us. They didn't even bother to warn us that they were losing money and were about to cut down on workers. They sprang it on us out of the blue."

"Yeah, that's the downside of a big conglomerate like that. They aren't personable these days." Elliot sighed as his lips quirked into a smile. "Is it bad that I'm kind of happy they fired you and that you're here now?"

Angela threw her head back in laughter. "Why? So you can boss me around and get some extra work done around here?"

"Maybe . . . But I like having the chance to spend time with you again. Not just a few days here and there throughout the year."

"I've been enjoying hanging out with you too. I never

realized how draining my old job was, and what it took from me emotionally and mentally, until recently."

Elliot watched his sister. She was revealing a part of herself he'd never seen before, a vulnerable side that was so unlike the strong, confident big sis he knew. "So, you're glad you got out of there?"

She lifted her chin, nodding slightly. "Yeah, I think I am."

A noisy ringtone broke their conversation, and Angela started to rummage through the pockets of the apron tied around her waist. Elliot crossed his arms as he narrowed his eyes at his sister. "I thought I told you no phones during work?"

Angela glanced up at him after peeking at the caller ID on her phone. "Oh, you were serious about that?"

"Yes, I was."

"Well, it's almost closing time, and this is about the job interview I had last week." She held up the phone for emphasis.

"The one Mr. Kiamichi got you?"

"That's the one. They said they'd call me once they'd made a decision."

Elliot looked at his watch and said, "Go ahead, you can take it. And good luck."

His sister mouthed a quick, "Thank you," before hustling over to the other side of the room to take the call. A hand fell on Elliot's shoulder, making him jump a bit before he realized Astrid was behind him.

"So jumpy," she said with a snicker.

"I wasn't expecting you to sneak up on me," Elliot said as he turned to face her. "What's up?"

"I was wondering about that girl you talked to last year. Think she's going to call you again this Christmas?"

Elliot felt something like anticipation well up inside him, mixed with a gnawing anxiety. "I'm not sure. She probably has plans or something. I doubt she's in the same place she was last year to warrant another conversation with a stranger."

"Many people's lives don't change that much within a year. Maybe you'll get lucky and hear that old rotary phone ring again."

"I doubt it, but if I do, I . . . won't be opposed to it."

Hanging up, Angela made her way back to where Elliot was standing and said, "What are you two chatting about?"

Astrid quickly answered, "Whether that woman he talked to last year will call him."

Her eyes widened. "I completely forgot about that." Angela turned to her brother and asked, "Was her name Summer, or June?"

Elliot gave a short chuckle and responded, "It's Autumn."

"Right . . ." She shook her head at her own memory slip before adding, "I hope she does give you a call, because she seemed to have quite an effect on you. Though I still think it's a little odd to fall for someone over the phone."

"I didn't fall for her. It was a pleasant conversation with a new friend who happens to live across the country. Like a pen pal, but—you know—through the phone."

She gave him a knowing smile. "Uh-huh. Well, whatever it is, I hope it continues."

"Okay, enough about me. What about your phone call?

Did you get the job?" When Angela sighed, a frown darkening her expression, Elliot felt a pang of pity for his sister. "Oh, I'm sorry."

But Angela's face quickly morphed into one of joy, a bright smile wiping away her frown. "I got the job. I start after New Year's."

Relief flooded Elliot, and he shook his head with a tight smirk. "I'm happy for you, but you didn't have to trick me like that."

"What fun would that be? But anyway, thanks. I'm excited to start doing some accounting work again."

Astrid chimed in, "That is fantastic, Angela. I guess we'll have to start looking for another employee. Let's not forget that Matt just graduated and got a job as the town's newest electrician. Without him, things will get a little hectic around here."

Elliot lowered his head as he squeezed the bridge of his nose with his forefinger and thumb. "Ugh, I didn't think about that. I'll have to post some listings online and put something in the newspaper to find a replacement for Matt."

"We can manage until then. We've done it before."

Elliot nodded, sucking in a calming breath. "I guess you're right. I'm sure Rosaline wouldn't mind taking a couple of extra shifts throughout the week until I find a new employee."

As Angela untied her apron, Astrid glanced at the watch on her left wrist and said, "Should we start closing up now, boss?"

Elliot checked the time on his phone. "Yeah, we can close up. It's already a couple of minutes after six, so the store is technically closed already."

"Great. I have a family gathering tonight, and we're having a white elephant gift exchange."

"Let me guess, you haven't picked out the gift yet?"

She winked. "They don't need to know that."

Angela chuckled and said, "That sounds like me. I almost always wait until the last minute to pick a gift up."

Elliot placed his hands on his hips, wearing a playful scowl. "Great, I run a shop with a bunch of procrastinators."

Angela nudged him with her elbow. "You should talk. I know for a fact that you've waited until the last minute for quite a few things, like your college application and filing your taxes."

"Okay," he admitted, "so I'm the head procrastinator of the bunch."

Astrid laughed and asked, "Hey, do you guys mind if I skedaddle? I mean, I can help clean up and set up for the twenty-sixth if you need me to."

Elliot shook his head and said, "No, we got this. Grab your white elephant gift and enjoy your holiday."

"Thanks. You too."

Astrid waved goodbye to the siblings before heading to the back to grab her things. Elliot turned to Angela and said, "You don't mind helping me close up shop, do you?"

"Not at all, little brother. Since I'll be leaving soon, I think it's the least I could do," Angela replied as she started to place the chairs upside down on top of the tables.

Elliot and his sister worked in sync as they tidied up the place. As they finished up, Elliot's mind drifted to the holiday tomorrow. Would Autumn actually call him like they promised, or did she have a busier and more exciting life to live now? He wasn't sure what the answer would be, but part of him hoped he'd receive a phone call on his great-grandmother's rotary phone on Christmas Day.

Chapter 10

Autumn

It was early Christmas morning, and as Autumn completed some prep work for the meal she was planning to whip up for Levi and herself, she noticed a few ingredients were missing. She was hesitant to go out, especially since it was in the low 30s today. As she continued to rummage through her cupboards, she finally heaved a sigh and decided to brave the frigid air, and swarms of other last-minute shoppers, to grab what she needed.

She drove to one of the stores in her neighborhood that stayed open for a few hours during the holiday. After grabbing the few ingredients she needed, she picked up another carton of eggnog since Levi would undoubtedly drink through the other carton in no time. As she purchased her items and shuffled out of the market, she kept her eyes on the wet pavement and ran into someone. Lifting her eyes, she saw the back of a tall man with a lean build. He turned, looking down at her, and her eyes widened when she caught sight of his pearly white smirk.

"Long time no see, Autumn," the all-to-familiar man crooned, his green eyes shimmering in the winter sun.

"Connor . . . Hi. I didn't expect to run into you here," she stammered with a faint smile on her lips.

"Small world."

Autumn's eyes were drawn to a woman with dusty blond hair draped over her left shoulder, who was sauntering toward them. The woman wrapped her arm around Connor's bicep. "Who's this, Con?"

"Uh, Linda, this is Autumn. She's my ex from college."

Linda nodded slowly. "Oh, I think you've mentioned her before."

The woman reached a dainty hand out for Autumn to shake. Autumn didn't want to be rude, so she shook it, but not without noticing the massive rock on her thin finger. When they pulled away, Autumn asked, "Are you two married?"

Linda smiled wide as she looked down to admire the ring. "We got married in May. It was a wonderful ceremony at my uncle's cottage."

Connor nodded as he pulled his wife close to him and said, "It sure was."

Autumn's heart throbbed with a dull pain as she stared back at the newlyweds. Connor had always told her that he wasn't the marrying type and wasn't planning on settling anytime soon. But now, the truth was clear. She just wasn't the one for him, and now four years later, he's happily married while she's married to her job. Autumn didn't want to make a fuss about it, so she mustered up a smile and said, "Congrats to you both. I'm happy for you, Connor."

"Thank you." Connor cocked his head to the side and asked, "Are you with anyone?"

"Not at the moment. I've had a lot of work lately, so I haven't had the time."

"I'm sure you'll find someone soon."

Linda chimed in. "I hate to cut this short, but we have to head down to my parents' house, and I don't want to be late. We just stopped to grab a pie and some cranberry sauce."

Autumn nodded and said, "I understand. It was nice seeing you again, Connor. And it was nice meeting you, Linda."

They said their goodbyes before heading in opposite directions. Autumn clambered into her car and just sat there with her hand on the wheel as she let the news sink in. Finally, she sucked in a quick inhale and took off to her apartment. When she arrived, Levi was waiting by her door, leaning against the wall with a few brightly wrapped presents in his arms. He put on a charming smile before it quickly turned into a frown. "Autumn, what's wrong? You're always so chipper this time of year."

"I ran into Connor when I went to the store," she answered as she fiddled with the key in the lock.

Levi sneered. "Not that weasel. Did he give you a hard time?"

"No, he introduced me to his new wife, though."

Levi helped hold the door for Autumn once she got it open, and as they stepped inside, he asked in a disbelieving tone, "He got married? How did someone like him get hitched before you?"

Autumn shrugged as she set her bags of groceries down on the counter and pulled them out so she could start cooking. "I have no idea. Apparently, he got married in May to a gorgeous blond."

He shook his head, looking repulsed. "I still say he cheated on you back in college. He was always so busy, and he was adamant about not being the marrying type."

She shrugged. "Maybe he just didn't connect with me."

"Sure, but he could have told you instead of stringing you along for three and a half years. He broke your heart, and it was on your birthday—which he didn't even remember."

Autumn looked down at the ham she was basting in a deep pan, the dread of that memory washing through her the moment Levi brought it up. "Can we drop this? I don't want to think about it."

Levi's shoulders sank as he gave her a little nod of understanding. "You're right. That should be left in the past, like it has been for the last four years. Today, we should be celebrating our friendship Christmas without any abysmal distractions."

She smiled to show her relief. "Thank you."

Autumn continued basting the ham before sliding it into the preheated oven she'd set prior to running to the store. She watched as Levi placed his presents under the tree and asked, "What'd you get me?"

Levi scoffed. "Like I'm really going to tell you. And don't you sneak a peek while I'm not looking."

"That only happened once, and we were thirteen. I think I've grown since then."

"Not by much," he said, patting the top of her head while sashaying to her refrigerator.

She crossed her arms in front of her chest. "You're so funny I forgot to laugh."

"Aw, come on. You know I love you."

Levi pulled out a carton of eggnog before grabbing two glasses from the cupboard. Placing the glasses on the counter, he poured a generous amount for each of them. They took their drinks to her couch and struck up a conversation.

"Are you calling that man today?" Levi asked as he peered over his glass.

Autumn shrugged, sipping her drink. "I was thinking about it. It wouldn't hurt to give him a call."

"Go for it, girl." He jumped from the couch and hopped over to the tree lit with hundreds of multi-colored lights. "So, can we open presents now? Because I'm dying to know what's in this oddly shaped one." He motioned to the bulky gift that was circular on one side and awkwardly wrapped.

"I'm sure you already know what it is."

Levi picked up said present, looking over the gaudy blue wrapping paper littered with cartoon snowmen and snow angels. He caressed the large portion that was spherical, yet almost triangular, then slipped his fingers along the slender brim underneath. He shook his head and said, "Well, it's not a steering wheel like I'd first thought."

Autumn rolled her eyes, a light chuckle leaving her lips. "Just open it, you big goober."

He tore through the thin paper with ease to reveal a charcoal-black fedora with a slim beige band around the trim. Levi feigned shock with his mouth agape and eyes wide, throwing a hand over his chest. "I'll be darned . . . It's a fedora. And a cute one at that."

"Try it on."

He placed the fedora atop his head, a bit of pizzazz going into every movement. He tipped the hat forward, giving his best friend a sultry wink, and asked, "How does it look, milady?"

"You've never looked gayer," she said with a genuine smile.

"I'll take that as a compliment," Levi replied as he hopped over to the small mirror hanging in her living room. "Ooh . . . I do make this look good. I'll have every man in the bar scrambling for me next time I go out."

"There is no doubt about that."

Levi grabbed another present from under the tree, a rectangular box with red wrapping paper featuring Christmas tree silhouettes. He handed the gift to Autumn, who raised an inquisitive eyebrow as she gently shook the box. "This is too heavy to be clothing."

He laughed as he sat next to her on the couch. "Maybe it's a set of clothes. Like a leather jacket, boots, some sexy skinny jeans, and a t-shirt."

"If that's the case, I'll happily exchange them for something I'll actually wear."

"Ugh . . . Rude. At least pretend you like it so you don't hurt my poor, poor feelings."

"Fine. I wouldn't want your feelings hurt." Autumn carefully unwrapped the present in her lap and found herself staring at a brand-new digital drawing tablet. She drew in a gasp delighted shock. "I thought we weren't getting each other anything fancy?"

Levi put an arm around her and said, "I know, but I was sure you wouldn't pick up a new one until yours kicked the bucket, which it literally is, might I add. Plus, they were on sale, and I couldn't pass up the chance to make your day."

She gave her friend a side hug, which was a little awkward because of the angle they were sitting on the couch. "Thank you. This will seriously speed up my process when I'm working on new designs."

"Great. I'm sure you'll need to sharpen your game with that new promotion."

She grazed a hand across the box. "Now I feel bad that I didn't get you something special."

"Don't fret. This is something I wanted to do for you, and your joy makes me happy."

She turned to him, tears pricking at her eyes. "You truly are the best, Levi."

"I know," he said with a shrug and sly smirk.

The went back to unwrapping presents, which mostly featured clothes, some household goods, and a couple of gag gifts. Once they were done, Autumn finished cooking their Christmas dinner while Levi chugged down most of the eggnog. After they sat down and enjoyed their meal together, chatting about old times, Levi headed home so Autumn could call Elliot.

Chapter 11

Elliot

Elliot lay sprawled back on the couch with his feet propped on the coffee table. A glass tumbler was nestled snugly in his hand as he sipped his spiked cider. Angela walked over to the couch, slapping his foot as she sat down beside him. "Get your feet off the furniture!"

"Who are you, our mother?" he retorted as he reluctantly removed his feet from the table.

"It's common courtesy." She glanced down at the drink in his hand and asked, "Isn't that your fourth one?"

"Fifth, but who's counting?"

"You should slow down on those; you're not getting any younger."

"As much as I love having you here for Christmas after

many years of lonely holidays, I do miss the quiet time I had to myself."

Angela gave her brother a stern look. "I'm only looking out for you. I know I'm only a guest here until I can get a place of my own, but I don't want to see you drowning your sorrows with booze."

He sighed. "I'm not doing that. Anyway, I barely drink on normal days. Holidays are the only time I make an exception and overindulge a little."

She raised her hands in surrender. "Okay, you got me there. But still, maybe cutting back a bit will do you some good. We don't want you to turn into Uncle Ray."

He scoffed. "Don't be ridiculous. I would never go down the road of Uncle Ray. From his marriage falling apart to losing all his hair and drinking nothing but alcohol from dusk till dawn every day. I am far from that nightmare."

"I'm just giving you some perspective," she murmured as she patted his shoulder. "So, she didn't call you, huh?"

Elliot peered over at the rotary phone before shaking his head. "I guess she was busy. And I mean, it's still only about six over on the West Coast."

"Then there's still hope, right?"

"I guess so, but I doubt she'll end up calling. She probably forgot, or she has better things to do than call a stranger she chatted with on the phone a year ago."

"Well, the holiday isn't over quite yet. Maybe she'll surprise you."

"Believe me, I'll be *very* surprised if she does." He looked over at his sister and asked, "How about you? How'd your chat with Remy go earlier?"

Her face lit up as she answered, "Great! He even said that

he would love to make a trip here for a change and let me be the tour guide for once."

He tried to suppress a smirk. "And you say you two aren't together?"

She chuckled. "We're friends. That's it."

"Let me get this straight. You want me to get with a girl who I've never met before, who is also over two thousand miles away. Yet you won't date a guy that's over three thousand miles away, who you've known for years, and who you clearly like?"

She scoffed and said, "First of all, I don't like Remy like that. He's a fantastic guy, but not someone I'd pursue romantically. Second, I never said you should 'get with her.' Obviously, she had an impact on you last Christmas, but it doesn't mean you two can't be just friends like Remy and me. It's nice to have someone else to talk to on rare occasions."

"Yeah, that's true. It was nice talking to someone new who didn't know my whole life story like most people in this town do."

"See? So, even if you don't want to date her, she'll do wonders for your mental health and getting stuff off your chest."

"That's if she calls."

Angela squeezed his leg and gave him a reassuring smile. "She'll call."

It seemed almost like fate, because the red rotary phone started to ring right after the words left her mouth. The annoying chime of the ringer carried through the house as Elliot said, "It's probably just our aunt and uncle."

"Only one way to find out." Angela stood from her place

on the couch and said, "I'll be in my room if you need me. You go get her, tiger."

Before he could reply, she was already halfway down the hall toward her room. Elliot walked over to the phone, clearing his throat as he placed his hand on the receiver. His heart was hammering in his chest as he picked it up. He didn't want to get his hopes up, but he desperately wanted to hear Autumn's voice on the other end. He let out a short breath before he said a simple, "Hello?"

A sweet, airy voice filled his ears, one that couldn't possibly come from his eighty-seven-year-old aunt. It had to be her. "Hi, is this Elliot?"

He forced his vocal cords to respond as casually as possible, "Yep, that's me. Is this Autumn?"

"Yes. I'm Autumn." She sounded amused.

He smiled shyly to himself. "I didn't think you'd call."

"I didn't think you'd answer, but I thought I'd give it a shot."

Elliot leaned against the round wooden table that held the phone, twirling the coiled red cable around his index finger. "Did you have any plans this Christmas?"

"Not really. I hung out with my friend for a bit, but he left a little while ago. How about you?"

"My sister was in town this year, so we got to spend our first Christmas together in a long time."

Her angelic voice hummed in acknowledgment on the other end. "You mentioned that your sister usually goes to Paris every year, right?"

"Yes. Sadly, she wound up losing her job and was forced to move back to Vermont."

"Oh, I'm sorry to hear that."

He gave a light shrug. "It's not too bad. Between you and me, I kind of like having her back in town."

"Well, your secret is safe with me."

Leaning one hand on the table, he asked, "How has life been for you since last year?"

Autumn let out a beautiful chuckle that rang like sleigh bells. "I mean no offense, because you're quite nice, but I probably wouldn't have called if my life had picked up in any way."

He struggled to control his own bout of laughter and said, "Okay, that's fair. I guess the same could be said about me."

"I did manage to score a small promotion at work. It's not the best, and I have almost doubled my workload, but I feel like I'm heading in the right direction."

"Hey, that sounds like a great step."

"So, did anything interesting happen to you this year?"

He sighed quietly. "Not really. One of my employees left to pursue a better job opportunity, and my sister will be leaving the café since she ended up getting a new job."

"That's rough."

"It's not ideal, but I'll make it work. I think this is the only time I've actually been thankful we don't get many customers coming in on a daily basis. With the three employees I have left, and myself, we can get the job done until a new employee comes along."

"You seem like you have it figured out."

"If there was one thing my father taught me before he passed, it was how to run our business. Hey, it might not be the best way or the right way, but it seems to work for us."

"Well, that's all that matters."

Elliot looked down at the hardwood-patterned laminate floor that contrasted beneath his white-socked feet. He continued to twirl the cable but sped up his motions as he thought about the suggestion he was going to make. He cleared his throat as he got ready to hit Autumn with a question that could make or break this newfound friendship. "What do you say about FaceTiming each other?"

"An actual face-to-face conversation?" she asked, clearly not expecting the invitation.

"I understand if you don't want to," he rushed out, "but I'd like to put a face to the person I'm talking to."

"I . . ." He could hear her hesitation on the other end. The only sound coming through was her faint breathing as she probably pondered the request. "I think that would be nice."

Elliot smiled as the butterflies in his belly were released from the cage of his clenched stomach. "Great! Why don't I give you my cell phone number? Just in case you have second thoughts, so you can be the one to make the call."

"That sounds good." He heard her shuffle about. "I got a pen and paper."

"Okay, here's my number." He spoke the digits slowly while she wrote them down.

"All right, got it. I'll give you a call shortly."

"I'm looking forward to it."

They said a quick goodbye before hanging up. Elliot grabbed his cellphone off the coffee table and dashed to his room at the other end of the house. He latched his door shut quietly and scrambled over to his dresser, above which hung a simple square mirror. He placed his phone down and raked his right hand through his dark-brown hair, trying to make it presentable to the woman he was about to meet. Come to think of it, he wasn't even sure if this lady looked at all the way he pictured her. She could have been a cougar, or maybe someone who has had a rough life on the streets. Or she could have been way out of his league.

He continued to gussy up whether she was drop-dead gorgeous or as hideous as a swamp witch—boils and all. Elliot fixed the collar on his navy-blue dress shirt before unbuttoning and re-buttoning the third-to-last button, trying to figure out what looked best. On his third re-buttoning, his cell phone chirped a deep triple chime, signaling that a FaceTime call was being requested. He sucked in a gulp of air, hollowing his cheeks before breathing it out. Once he grabbed his phone, his thumb hovered over the answer button as he got his bearings. Pushing aside his hesitation, he slid the button to the right and answered the call.

The image that popped up on his screen completely derailed his train of thought. He had been hoping for someone decent looking, and not as old as his sister, but he was floored by the young woman before him. He took a moment to observe the girl who had stolen his thoughts since last Christmas. Her medium-tan skin seemed to shimmer under the yellow-toned lights shining down on her. Her choppy, dark-brown pixie cut made her slightly rounded facial features stand out in the most delightful way. The last feature Elliot admired was Autumn's almond-shaped eyes, which were a deep brown color. But the way the light was hitting them, they seemed to harbor small flakes that sparkled like honey.

Autumn's face contorted into one of confusion, and Elliot noticed her fingers fidgeting with her phone. "Are we frozen? Can you hear and see me?"

Elliot snapped out of the trance he'd found himself in and shook his head at the screen. "No, we're good. I can see you."

"Great! thought I lost you for a second." She gave him a cute lopsided grin, but he could tell she was nervous. Then again, so was he. "You know what?" she continued, "You're not at all how I expected you'd look."

"I don't know if that's good or bad. Am I at least better looking than what you thought?"

She beamed. "Most definitely. I honestly thought you'd be an older man going through a midlife crisis."

"Do I sound that old over the phone?" he asked with an anxious chuckle.

"Not at all. But I've met older men that still sounded young, so you never know what to expect."

"I can't argue with that. Honestly, I didn't know what to expect either."

"We were both pretty wary, huh?"

"Yeah, but I think we had every right to be. Who knows what kind of creeps are out there?"

"I guess you're right," she said, glancing down. Elliot watched as Autumn thought about what to say next. "How old are you, anyway? If you don't mind me asking."

"Not at all," Elliot said, shooting her a quick smile. "I'm thirty-one. How about yourself?"

"I'll be twenty-nine in a few months."

He cocked his head. "You don't look that old at all."

"Thanks. I get that a lot. There have been so many times I've met with a client, and they assumed I was the intern."

"Oh, Wow . . ." His mind drifted to their previous conversation. "You're an interior decorator, right?"

"That I am."

"How have things been at your job? Besides the promotion, that is."

She shrugged and said, "Not too bad. Since the promotion, I've been getting a lot more work from my boss. Which I don't mind, since I love decorating clients' homes and businesses. The only thing that really bothers me is being around the boss's son."

Elliot nodded as he scratched at the short stubble on his face. "What's wrong with him?"

She frowned, her brow furrowing as though she were trying to find the right words. "Well, he's just . . . a tad annoying. He's always hitting on me and stealing my ideas, making them his own."

"That doesn't seem right."

"I know, but there's not much I can do about it, except turn his advances down and be grateful that my ideas are being used, even if I'm not the one getting credit for them."

"Have you told your boss?"

Autumn's dark eyes widened, and she gasped. "No way! If I tell her anything remotely negative about her son, I'll be fired."

"Hmm . . . Too bad. You shouldn't have to work with someone you don't like, even if it is the boss's son."

"Thankfully, it's not often. Even though we work on the

same floor now, I don't have to see him as much as I used to."

"Well, as long as you're happy overall." Elliot shifted on his bed to get more comfortable and asked, "So, how was your holiday? I know you mentioned your friend came over to visit."

"Yeah, he's been my best friend since middle school, and we've spent countless holidays together. This year we decided to hang out and exchange some gifts. So it wasn't too bad. Though, I did run into my ex from college—along with his new wife."

"I bet that was rough."

She looked thoughtful for a moment. "It just really took me by surprise. He was very adamant about not wanting to settle down, but as it turns out, he did want to. Just not with me. I should have known, though. He was always distant, and he was rarely around during our three years together. The worst part is he broke up with me on my birthday, which he completely forgot about."

Elliot felt a swell of indignance on her behalf. "Seems like you dodged a bullet."

Autumn gave him a hint of a smile. "I guess I did."

"Speaking of exes, my high school-slash-college sweetheart is about to get married to one of our classmates next spring. I'm still trying to decide whether I want to go."

"They invited you to the wedding?"

"We've all known each other since preschool. And the breakup was pretty amicable, so I'd feel bad if I didn't go and support her. Plus, it's a small town, so whether I go or not, people will talk."

"I guess that's one of the cons of living in a small town."

"Oh yeah. Like anything, there's always going to be upsides and downsides."

"Well, I think you should go if you're all still friends."

"That's my current plan. I just wish I had a plus-one."

"I would offer to go, but for one, it might be a little early for a wedding date. And then there's the fact that we're thousands of miles away. That doesn't help."

"Well, I appreciate the thought. I'm sure going stag won't be too bad."

She wiggled her eyebrows. "Maybe you'll get all the ladies."

He snorted and said, "Doubtful. I've known most of them since we were in diapers, so I don't think they'd be falling for me now."

Autumn let out a snicker and replied, "Weird things happen at weddings."

"Talking from experience?"

"No . . . But the friend I was telling you about? I've seen him go home with plenty of phone numbers and men at the weddings we've attended together. Some of the men I could have even *sworn* were straight."

Elliot felt some relief wash over him when he realized that her close friend wasn't and wouldn't be pursuing her. He didn't want any competition for Autumn, even if they may never end up together. He still wanted to hold onto hope, just in case they ever could meet and fall in love. "Oh, wow," he teased. "So, you're saying I have a chance, and quite possibly might get picked up by another guy?"

Autumn burst into a fit of laughter, the sound making Elliot's heart swell. When she regained her composure, she said, "I mean, it could happen."

"I guess I can't be too picky these days."

She nodded. "The dating pool is only getting smaller."

"Isn't that the truth."

Hours later, they were still chatting away, just like last Christmas. They talked about everything they could think up. From what happened within the last 365 days since they last talked to their fondest and funniest childhood memories. Elliot had been so sure that last year was a fluke. That there was no way he and Autumn would be able to talk with such ease and excitement once again. But here they were. Their conversation seemed so fluid, and each story they told led to the next flawlessly. He just wished they could converse in person instead of through their devices. At least modern technology let them see each other from thousands of miles away.

As their conversation began to wind down, Elliot let out a yawn, quickly covering his mouth with his free hand. Autumn let out a light-hearted chuckle and joked, "Am I boring you?"

"Not at all," he said, releasing a hearty laugh of his own. "I guess I'm just getting tired since it's nearing midnight over here. I haven't stayed up this late in a while, so my body is telling me that it's time to get some shut-eye."

"Oh, yeah. It is getting quite late."

"If I didn't have to open the shop tomorrow, even though the twenty-sixth is usually a slow day, I'd talk to you until sunrise. But I still need to be consistent for those customers who do show up."

"I should probably get going too. I have a meeting with a client tomorrow that I need to get ready for."

Before Autumn could say goodbye, Elliot blurted, "Hey, can I suggest something crazy?"

Autumn gave Elliot a puzzled look. "What is it?"

He ran a hand through his hair as he composed himself. He wasn't sure if she'd be up for his idea, but it wouldn't hurt to ask. "I was thinking . . . that maybe we don't have to wait until Christmas to talk to each other again. Now that we've seen each other and have exchanged numbers, it might be nice to have someone else to talk to besides the few friends and family I have here."

Her smile could have lit up the Rockefeller Center Christmas Tree. "That's not such a bad idea. I'd love to talk with you some more, and it would be nice not waiting until Christmas."

"I agree. You can never have too many friends to chat with."

"That is true." Autumn hummed and asked, "Is there a best time to contact you?"

He shook his head. "Any time is good for me, especially during the weekends. But any time after 6 p.m., I'm more likely to answer the phone."

"I'll keep that in mind. My schedule varies depending on the project I'm working on. But you could always call and leave a message, and I'll call back when I can."

"Sure thing." Elliot gave his newfound friend a bright smile. "Thanks for talking with me, Autumn. I had a great time with you."

"I had a good time too," she replied with a smile of her

own.

"I'll talk to you again soon, I hope."

"I hope so too."

They said their goodbyes before ending the FaceTime call. Elliot fell backward onto his bed with an elated sigh. He wasn't sure what this thing with Autumn was, or what it may amount to in the future. But he was going to enjoy it while it lasted, especially if she did call beyond just Christmas time.

2019

Chapter 12

Autumn

April

Autumn rushed around her office, trying to collect her paperwork and diagrams that were scattered about the room, which was reasonably bigger than her old office. Some sheets were lying on the extra-plush visitor seats while others were strewn on her large, round work table that sat across from her desk. She grabbed the papers she needed to make changes to, quickly rolling them into the thinnest cylinders she could form, so she could stuff them in the smallest number of tubes to take home.

"Have a hot date with your phone guy?" Levi's voice rose behind her.

She glanced over to where he stood at the doorway to her office, leaning against the black frame. She impaled him with an unamused glare as she continued to gather her belongings. "It's not a date. He doesn't even know I'll be calling him."

"Whatever you say. I don't blame you for keeping that man in your life. Those screenshots you showed me the day after your Christmas FaceTime? Quite impressive. His baby blues and chiseled jaw—whew!"

"How many times do I have to tell you that the two of us are just friends? It'll never go beyond that." She tried to ignore the blush sneaking up her cheeks.

"Right . . . You two are just 'phone pals,' as you like to put it. Nothing more."

"Yep. That's it. It's therapeutic to get things off my chest with someone who is basically a stranger."

"I don't think you two qualify as strangers anymore. This is like your fourth phone call with the guy since that fateful Christmas mix-up. So, I'd say more like acquaintances."

"Well, whatever he may be, our chats are a great pastime that helps me destress from work. Besides the time you and I spend together, of course."

Levi sauntered over to Autumn and raised a knowing eyebrow. "Come on. You know you're infatuated with the guy."

Autumn plopped down in her leather office chair and grumbled, "Fine, you win. I'll admit I've got it bad . . . But at the same time, I know I'll never be able to go out with him. At least not in the way I'd like to."

"I get it, I truly do. But you never know. Maybe he winds

up expanding his coffee shop business and opens up a franchise right here in Seattle. Meanwhile, you continue to make your way up the ladder in the agency, taking the design world by storm with your intricate décor ideas."

"Sure, maybe in my fantasies. Come on, Levi, that'll never happen."

He lifted his chin in a confident pose. "I like to think it will. All I want is to see my best friend happy, and this guy has clearly been doing a stellar job of that so far."

She offered him a warm smile. "Thanks, Levi. I appreciate your positivity, and your concern for my well-being. Maybe I'll borrow some of that hope you have and wish for a miracle that Elliot and I could wind up together."

He returned her smile. "That's the spirit."

"Knock. Knock," came the annoying voice of Rodney as he entered the room with the overconfident swagger he always wore. "I need to talk to you for a split second, Autumn."

"What is it?" she asked, struggling to muster up a friendly smile.

"Alone," Rodney said as he peered over at Levi.

"I'll see you tomorrow, Autumn." Levi shot a quick glower at the man beside him. "Rodney."

Rodney hummed, barely acknowledging his other coworker. Once Levi was gone, Rodney dove into the business he was evidently there to discuss. "Listen. You've been working here for some odd years now, right?"

"Almost seven, but who's counting?" she said as she crossed her arms.

"So then, you know about the summer banquet held

every year at the Seattle Garden Country Club."

"It's only the second biggest event in the States for interior designers and decorators. Of course I know about it," she spat back.

"Well, then you'd know my mother and her company are invited practically every year."

"Yes, I'm aware. What's this have to do with me?"

"Not so much you, but all of us here at Lamour's Interior Decorating Company. We were selected to host the fine event this year. And best of all, you and I will be in charge of decorating the banquet hall of the country club."

Autumn's eyebrows shot up as she processed this news. One of the biggest events after the award ceremony held in New York every January, and their company had just received the honor of hosting it? This could be the big break she was looking for. Everyone who is anyone in the interior design and home decorating business would be there. Even though this meant working with Rodney once again, an opportunity like this wasn't one to be passed up just because of an annoying coworker.

"Your stunned silence is telling me that maybe you're not the right person for the job." He started shuffling toward the door at an agonizingly slow pace. "I could always ask Hailey, Kiki, or Ralph to join me. Maybe even that Davidson fellow you're friends with."

Autumn held her right hand up, gesturing for him to stop. Rodney obviously knew she wanted to work the gig, but it wouldn't be him if he didn't torture her before handing her the opportunity. "I would like to decorate the banquet hall with you, if I can."

"Are you sure? I don't want you to be too swamped."

"Rodney . . . Come on."

"What's the magic word?"

Autumn groaned, wishing she could just refuse to answer this arrogant man. But at the same time, she really wanted this chance to show what she was made of. "Please," she said through gritted teeth.

"There it is," Rodney said as he flashed his pearly whites. "We'll check out the banquet hall next Wednesday around one in the afternoon. We could carpool from work if you'd like?"

She glared back. "I'm not getting in your death trap of a car."

"All vehicles are death traps if you think about it. But we could always take my Jaguar if you'd prefer."

She wore a tight-lipped smile. "I'll think about it."

"See you tomorrow."

With a quick wave, Rodney left the room, and Autumn remained seated in her office chair, too shocked to do anything else. She couldn't believe it. She was going to be a part of the décor crew for the Interior Design and Décor Banquet! But now the pressure was on—all the big names would be judging her style and creativity. If this went down in history as one of the worst of the event's forty-year run, she'd never work another day in her life in this industry. And she knew Rodney wouldn't get a single ounce of the blame for it. This whole thing would be riding on her shoulders, and suddenly, she was feeling a bit nauseous at the thought of it all.

Autumn stepped into her apartment at around seven o'clock and scarfed down a quick microwave meal of broccoli fettuccine alfredo. After cleaning herself up a bit, she threw on some comfortable clothes so she could look presentable yet relaxed during her video call with Elliot. She sprawled on her couch, propping herself up with her elbow on the armrest. Her legs were carefully tucked beside her, brushing against the back cushion lazily. Once she was situated, she opened up the FaceTime app and dialed Elliot's number.

The phone rang briefly before his tired face filled the screen. Autumn couldn't help but notice Elliot's drooping eyes with dark bags beneath them, and he immediately let out a monstrous yawn that he covered with his hand. Autumn felt a twinge of guilt for not texting him first, not realizing until this moment that it was almost a quarter to midnight on the East Coast. "I'm sorry, Elliot. You must have been sleeping."

"No, I was just resting my eyes," he said unconvincingly as he rubbed his left eye with the back of his hand.

"No, really. I shouldn't have called so late. I'll just ring you up over the weekend."

"Seriously, don't worry about it. I'd love to chat with you tonight."

A smile teased her lips. "If you say so."

"So, what warranted this spontaneous phone call, anyhow?"

"Well, I got some wonderful news today at my job."

His face perked up. "Nice. Can you tell me about it?"

"Of course." Autumn brightened as her mind went to the exciting opportunity that was coming up in a few months. "You see, every year since about the mid-1970s, there's a big banquet in Seattle where elite interior designers and decorators from around the world come to mingle and share new designs. A few awards are given out as well. It's the best place to get noticed and gather new ideas."

"Have you attended this thing before?"

"No, never. I'm not even close to getting the honor of receiving an invite."

His brow wrinkled in obvious confusion. "So, why are you excited about it this year?"

"I'm going to have the chance to showcase my decorating skills at the event, because our company was tasked with setting up the banquet hall."

A surprised smile spread across Elliot's face. "Wow! That sounds awesome."

"It is, but now the nerves are setting in. This is the biggest event in the Seattle area, hosting the best of the best in the interior design-slash-decorating industry. If I make any mistakes, I could kiss my career goodbye."

"Don't put so much pressure on yourself. I'm sure you'll come up with the most tasteful decoration setup they've ever seen."

"I sure hope so." Autumn's shoulders drooped as her happy thoughts were invaded by the other factor that would make the project a living nightmare. "It doesn't help that I'll be working with my boss's son, Rodney, on this project."

"Oh, that's the guy who you don't like, right? He's the creep with no boundaries."

She scoffed. "That's the one. He's not bad at his job, but

he does have a habit of taking others' ideas and calling them his own. Not to mention the advances he makes on almost every woman he sees."

"He does sound like a pain to work with," Elliot mentioned. "Hopefully he doesn't bother you too much as you work on decorating for the event. It'd be awful to lose out on an opportunity so amazing because of some jerk."

"You're right. I shouldn't let him get to me, especially with something like this on the line," she said, feeling a notch more confident. "How about you? How was your day?"

Elliot chuckled. "Not as eventful as yours."

"Nothing interesting going on with the café?"

"Nope. Same routine as usual. Though I did get fitted for the tuxedo that I'll be wearing to my ex's wedding."

"Hey, that's something. So, you're actually going?"

"I think I am. We're all old friends, so why not be there to show them my support? Plus, if I go to the reception, I don't have to cook that night."

"Hey, a free dinner is definitely worth it."

"I agree."

She giggled before asking, "So, are you bringing a plus-one or going stag?"

"I'm bringing my sister. Not exactly who I had in mind for my wedding date, but she did used to babysit most of us as kids, so I think it's fitting to bring her along. She'll know most of the people there."

"That actually sounds like fun."

"I'm hoping it will be. I just pray no unnecessary drama arises from me being there."

"You know there will be that one person who brings it up, but hopefully not enough for everyone to be able to dust it off and ignore it, so it's a happy day all around."

"Yeah, we'll see."

Autumn checked the time on her phone, shocked to see that it was almost eleven her time, which meant it was almost two in the morning his time. She figured he'd want to get some sleep, so she said, "Thanks for letting me chat with you this late. I'll let you go."

"Not a problem," he said, a yawn trying to break through his words. "I'll happily stay up for you whenever you need to talk."

"I'd do the same."

"Have a good night, Autumn."

"You too, Elliot. I'll talk to you again soon."

She hung up and smiled to herself. It was at times like these that she wished Elliot didn't live across the country. She was sick of worrying about time differences. Not to mention, it would be nice to talk in person instead of interacting via a pixelated screen and lagging audio. But she was grateful to have another friend to share stories and milestones with. Maybe someday soon, she'd find someone else to chat with who was close by, but for now, this was good enough for her.

Chapter 13

Elliot

May

Elliot fussed with the silky mint-hued bow tie currently draped over his neck. Every time he started tying the unruly fabric, halfway through the process, everything either fell apart or the end product wound up looking like a contorted balloon animal from a five-year-old's birthday party. He never imagined tying a bow tie would be this frustrating. Usually, he either relied on clip-ons or stuck with a simple necktie.

He made one more attempt, but once again, his fingers and the bow tie refused to work together, and he was stuck with a jumbled mess. Just when he was about to give up, his sister swooped in next to him and started tying the matte fabric like a pro. With finesse, she looped one end, folded a couple of the sections, and pulled the ribbon of fabric through the final hole. Elliot glanced in the mirror, relieved that he now had a dapper and symmetrical bow tie to show off at the wedding. He glanced down at his sister, offering her a grateful smile. "Thanks for that. I was just about to give up on this look and fall back on a necktie."

"Anything for my little brother. I *am* surprised you don't know how to tie a bow tie, though," Angela said with a short chuckle. "You know, there are tutorial videos online for this type of thing."

"Mastering bow-tying skills was never a priority for me. And I was too frustrated to stop and search YouTube, especially since we're already running late."

"Don't worry, I'm sure the wedding won't start on time anyway. And we get to make a fashionable entrance to your ex's wedding. That should get some heads turning."

Elliot grabbed his slate gray blazer from where it hung on the bedpost. "That's the last thing I want. I'm already going to have people talking; I don't want to give them more reason to gossip."

"Well, I think the whole thing is silly. You two have been broken up for years and people should let it go. But I do understand your point." Angela sauntered out of the room, and without turning back to her brother, she said, "Let me get my cardigan and purse, and I'll meet you at the car."

"Sure. I'll get it started."

He was about to exit his bedroom, but at the last minute, he decided to snap a picture in the full-length mirror he'd recently installed behind his bedroom door. After shutting his door halfway, he took a few snapshots with his phone, hoping at least one of them turned out halfway decent. As he made his way to his pick-up truck, he sent a text to Autumn asking how he looked, along with the best of his mirror selfies. While he waited for his sister to hop in, so they could drive to the cottage wedding venue, a text from Autumn came through. *"You look fantastic, Mr. 007!"*

"I'm not as suave as Mr. Bond, and neither is my suit, but I'll take that compliment," he replied.

"Have a blast at the wedding. I hope nothing crops up because of your shared past and that it's a fun, drama-free night."

"Thanks, I'm going to need it. But don't worry, you'll hear all about it either tonight or tomorrow."

Autumn sent back a thumbs-up emoji, but before he could write anything back, Angela was clambering into the truck. He slipped his phone into the inside pocket of his blazer as his sister teased, "Your mood seems to have taken a turn for the better. Just look at that boyish grin on your face. Were you chatting with that long-distance crush of yours?"

Elliot flicked his eyes toward his sister as he started to back out of the driveway. "Maybe . . . and she's not my crush, just a friend."

She gave him a poorly hidden smirk. "You could have fooled me. Every time you talk to that girl, your whole face seems to brighten, and you become the young Elliot who was excited about everything."

"What can I say? She brings out the best in me. There's nothing wrong with that."

"You're right. I guess Remy does the same for me when

we chat or hang out."

He cast her a quick glance of victory. "See? So there's nothing weird about it."

"Duly noted."

They continued their drive toward the venue, which lay just outside of their little town where the last wooded neighborhoods skirted the countryside. As Elliot drove, the anxiety started to kick in. He couldn't help but dread what might be awaiting him at one of the most impactful weddings of his adulthood.

They arrived at the rustic cottage venue only a couple of minutes late. Thankfully for Elliot, there were still a handful of people meandering outside the front doors and in the parking lot. He and Angela approached the usher, who was directing the attendees to their seating areas. The young man, looking to be in his early twenties, led them to the clearing behind the cottage where a spacious lawn of lush grass was lined with dozens of white folding chairs, cream-colored cushions adorning their seats. A pastel-purple ribbon was elegantly tied on the back of each chair. Elliot had known purple was Sophia's favorite color since elementary school, so he wasn't surprised to see the whimsical shade sprinkled throughout the venue. At the end of the center aisle was a large white arch carved with intricate designs that weaved in and out of each other as they crawled the sides. Two showy flower arrangements featuring lavender, white, and yellow blooms wrapped around the front and back of the arch, giving it a beautiful fairy-tale look.

The usher motioned with his right hand toward the two sides of the aisle and said, "The right side is for guests of the groom while the left is for the bride. We're running a bit late, but it should be starting soon. Enjoy the ceremony."

The young usher hustled away, probably to help other guests, and Elliot looked around for a spot to sit. Angela nudged him, leaning in close so he could hear her over the clamor. "So, are we sitting on your ex's side or your old school friend's side?"

Elliot gestured to the seats on the left. "I guess Sophia's, since I know her better. Hudson and I were never that close."

"I suppose we'll be sitting toward the back since most of the guests have already staked a claim on the seats."

Elliot quickly examined the crowded front and the vacant chairs near the back. "That's fine by me. I already feel eyes boring into my back, and I don't need any more during the ceremony."

Angela grabbed Elliot's hand and guided him toward a couple of unoccupied seats in the back row. They sat down next to another man and woman who seemed to be eagerly waiting for the wedding to start. The man next to Angela turned to study them, and Elliot instantly recognized the crooked smile and shifty brown eyes. "Elliot Lawson, long time no see."

"Jimmy Mondano . . ." he said, deciding to indulge in the conversation with his old classmate, although to be fair, he really had no other choice.

"I'm surprised you're not the one who'll be standing at

the altar with Soph'. You two were inseparable, and you took the cutest shots for the couples' section in our senior yearbook."

He forced a smile. "Things just didn't work out. No big deal."

"I guess so." Jimmy tapped the woman on his left and pointed toward Elliot. Turning back to Elliot, he said, "By the way, this is my fiancée, Roma. We met while I was doing some work in Jersey."

"Nice to meet you," Elliot said, offering a polite wave to the woman with hazel eyes and short chestnut hair. "Congrats to you both."

"Thank you," she whispered, seeming a bit reserved as she probably tried to figure out who he was.

Jimmy patted her back and said, "Oh, I went to school with this guy. Hung out once in a while, too, and got into some small-town teenage shenanigans."

"Ah, well that's nice."

Jimmy turned to Angela on his other side and said, "I see you brought your sister along." Addressing her, he went on, "I remember you babysitting me from time to time. I got away with a lot less with you than with my parents."

"Nice to see you too, Jimmy. I hope you're not as much of a handful as you were when you were little," Angela said with a brow raised.

"Well, ah, my parole officer would have to say I've still got that mischievous side, but I've been a good boy as of late. Especially since I have Roma here. She helped me turn my life around."

Angela's face softened. "That's good to hear. I hope everything goes well for you two."

"Thank you."

Before any more could be said, gentle music began to play, and the officiator and groom took their places at the front of the altar. Hudson stood tall, his head nearly grazing the top of the arch as he towered over the priest. His blond hair was slicked back with gel, and his black tux featured a splash of color with his lavender bow tie and matching pocket square. Soon, bridesmaids and groomsmen were waltzing down the aisle in outfits that perfectly matched the purple theme that was prominent throughout the décor. Once the cute flower girl, who couldn't have been more than four, skipped down the aisle, everyone stood to watch Sophia be escorted to the altar by her father.

Elliot's heart stopped as he caught sight of his ex in a tight-fitting, pearl-white dress that showed off all of her curves and features in an elegant, tasteful way. Her shoulders peeked out from the lacy sleeves that fell partially off the shoulder and extended down to the tops of her wrists. A short veil atop her vintage-styled hair completed the look, making her appear almost angelic. He didn't think he'd become jealous. After all, he'd been over her for several years now, but at this moment, some of those old feelings came flooding back. But Elliot knew she was no longer his, and he had to let her go. He caught her light-blue eyes flitting toward him, a secret smile gracing her face as she gave him a shadow of a nod. He returned it without a second thought.

Once Sophia was handed off to Hudson and her father sat down in the front row, the ceremony got underway. The priest started to speak, reciting the wedding script he'd probably learned when he got ordained. For the most part, it was silent in the verdant lawn, with a handful of guests crying or whispering to a neighboring attendee.

When the priest reached the dreaded phrase, "Should anyone present know of any reason that this couple should not be joined in holy matrimony, speak now or forever hold your peace," a few heads in the crowd turned to Elliot. He could feel the eyes burning into him, but he ignored their gazes, instead staring down at the grass below him. He could feel his cheeks warming up as he waited patiently for the vows to be read and the ceremony to wrap up. Thankfully, he didn't have to wait long as the wedding was quickly coming to a close.

Hudson and Sophia kissed to conclude their marriage ceremony. As they walked down the aisle arm in arm, many guests clapped for the newlywed couple while others wiped tears away. Elliot settled on clapping, feeling honestly happy for his ex-girlfriend and schoolmate. Maybe one day, he'd be lucky enough to have a wedding of his own with someone he truly loved.

The reception was to take place a short drive from the cottage, and it didn't take long for most attendees to begin flooding into the venue. Elliot and Angela found their assigned seats on a list that was posted outside the sizable banquet hall before stepping inside. The couple had a table set up for gifts as soon as guests walked in, and Elliot dropped off the heavy gift he had bought. Which happened to be an espresso maker, since he knew Sophia loved her coffee. He hoped the new couple would get plenty of use out of it.

The place was adorned with streamers, fairy lights, and gaudy bouquets, the décor sticking to the color scheme of purple and white. He saw that guests were already getting a jumpstart on the open bar, and Elliot didn't hesitate to join them. After receiving a glass of beer from the bartender, he made his way back to his sister, who was chatting up a few guests seated with them. Before he could make it to the table, Mr. Nolan stepped in front of him, his arms crossed. Elliot gulped as he stared down his ex's dad and suddenly felt like a teen again. Pushing his nerves aside, he gave the older man a gentle smile and said, "Nice to see you again, Mr. Nolan."

"You're due for a checkup. Three years past due, actually," was all the man said.

"Oh, uh . . . I'll make sure to book my appointment soon."

"I'm kidding. Kind of. You *are* due to get your teeth checked." With a snicker, Mr. Nolan smacked the side of Elliot's free arm. Though his carefree attitude soon took a solemn turn when he noticed the drink in Elliot's other hand. Mr. Nolan nodded toward the alcoholic beverage and said, "I see you're still drinking."

"I've cut down quite a lot. I'm not the same kid I was back in college, believe me."

"Good to hear. You've done all right, and you've been running your dad's café well. He'd be proud."

Elliot felt a swell of warmth in his chest. "Thank you. That means a lot."

Mr. Nolan sighed and said, "I'm honestly shocked that

you showed up today, but I'm sure my little girl is relieved that you came. She always cared about you, and she wouldn't have wanted you to miss this important day."

Elliot placed his empty hand in the pocket of his slacks and said, "I hold nothing against Sophia or Hudson, and I know they're a better match than we ever were. I wanted to support them."

Mr. Nolan cast his eyes down with a guilty look. "You know, I never gave you the benefit of the doubt, but at that time, I felt no man was good enough for my only child. You're a good guy, though, and I'm sure you'll find the right person for you soon."

Mr. Nolan patted his shoulder before heading off to mingle with other guests. Elliot didn't know how to take that conversation, but part of him felt as though a weight had been lifted off his shoulders. He never thought he'd get any kind of approval or acknowledgment from his ex's stern father, but here it was. He wished it could have come sooner, but maybe the delayed gratification was for the best.

He finished his stroll back to the table and sat next to Angela, who turned to him and asked, "What did Mr. Nolan say?"

"My teeth are due for a checkup," Elliot said, taking a sip of his beer.

"You're kidding."

"No, he really did. Then he told me that Dad would be proud. He also thinks I've turned out to be a decent man, and he wishes he'd seen it sooner."

Her eyes widened. "Huh, unexpected, but Mr. Nolan was always an interesting guy." Angela looked down at his drink and said, "Guess I'm driving us home."

He gave her an exasperated glare. "It's only one."

"Yes, but you're still impaired. Plus, I think a couple of more wouldn't hurt after watching your ex get married."

"I'm fine, but I guess I wouldn't mind a couple more," Elliot said as he handed his keys over to Angela.

"I know you are, but it doesn't hurt to indulge a little, at least for today. Just pace yourself. We don't need you hitting on Sophia and telling her that you're still madly in love with her at her own reception."

Elliot let out a laugh and said, "I don't think I will, but I'm sure you'll stop me if it comes to that."

"Stop you? Oh, I'd want to watch the drama unfold."

He narrowed his eyes playfully. "Of course you would."

They continued laughing and chatting as they waited for the food to be served and the reception events to begin. Eventually, the buffet was brought out to the back of the banquet hall, and people gradually trickled back to pick out their preferred dishes for dinner. When Elliot reached the buffet, he decided to get a little of everything because he couldn't decide what he wanted from the large spread. He served himself a few shrimp, the smallest filet of salmon, and a modest hunk of grilled chicken along with some vegetables and a small plate of salad. Angela stuck with the seafood items, pasta salad, and some roasted vegetables for her dinner, but she didn't hesitate to pick off Elliot's plate to sample any contents she didn't pick up.

After the scrumptious dinner, a few humorous and tearful toasts, dancing, and cake, the bride and groom started to mingle with the guests. Elliot was eager to congratulate them on the wedding so he could leave. Not that he wasn't having a great time, but he still felt awkward being there. Not many people acknowledged him, and those who did seemed to gloss over the fact that it could have been him. It wasn't as bad as he'd built it up in his mind to be, but he also didn't want to overstay his welcome.

Sophia and Hudson finally made their way over to him and Angela. He gave them both a quick hug and said, "I'm very happy for you both. Congrats on the wedding."

"Thanks, bro!" Hudson said as he lightly punched Elliot's right shoulder, making him wince. "I'm glad you came out."

Sophia nodded in agreement. "Me too. This made my day."

Elliot shrugged his left shoulder. "I wouldn't have missed it."

"I'm happy you came too, Angela," Sophia mentioned, giving his sister a sweet smile. "I remember when you used to babysit me and braid my hair. We had a lot of fun."

"Yes, I always loved babysitting you. Hudson as well," Angela said, smiling at the newlyweds. "You two make a lovely couple."

They said their thanks in unison, letting out a giddy chuckle at their matching timing. Hudson jutted his chin toward Elliot and said, "I have to thank you, man. If you hadn't let her go, then we wouldn't be here right now."

The happy atmosphere quickly turned sour, and Sophia mumbled, "Hudson, not now."

"What did I say? It's the truth."

Elliot shook his head and forced a charming grin. "He's

right. This wouldn't have happened if I hadn't let you go. But I'm glad it worked out for you both."

"I guess so." Sophia pulled at Hudson's arm while casting them one last, grateful look. "Thanks again for coming, Elliot and Angela. We have a lot more people to talk to, so we better keep moving before it gets too late."

They said their goodbyes, and soon, Elliot and Angela were on their way home. From the driver's seat, Angela finally ventured, "Are you glad you gave Sophia up?"

Elliot looked over to his sister, who kept her eyes on the road and her hands firmly on the wheel. "I wouldn't say 'glad.' Do I wish it worked out with the both of us? Sure. But it didn't, and this is where we are now."

After a short silence, she said, "You know, you never told me why you broke up."

"There's nothing to tell. It was right around the time Dad died, then Mom got sick. I had a lot piled on my plate, all within the span of a few months, and I needed time to myself. I thought it'd be best if we went on a break, and that short break turned into a long one, until we eventually figured we'd never get back together."

"Oh, I didn't know that." Angela sighed. "I think you did the right thing, Elliot. It might have ended much worse if you'd tried to make it work."

"I think so too."

They both went quiet as they made their way back to their childhood home. Elliot shot a quick text to Autumn, hinting that he'd tell her all about the wedding the next morning. He was too exhausted to hold a conversation tonight, and a good night's sleep seemed to be in order after this grueling day.

Chapter 14

Autumn

July 5ᵗʰ

Autumn stood at the center of the empty banquet hall. She was visiting the country club that was hosting the glamorous interior decorating and design event in a few weeks, hoping to scope out the place. Eying the venue, she noted that it was significantly bigger than she remembered from her first walk-through back in April. She'd need to make adjustments to some of her original plans.

"Don't you just love this place?" Rodney whispered in her ear from behind, making her jump. He snickered as he stepped into her field of view, looking full of himself in his striped dress shirt and black slacks. "A bit jumpy, are we?"

Autumn glared at the man and gritted out, "You're late, like always."

"I had some business to take care of."

"Business, or pleasure?"

"Maybe a bit of both," he said as the side of his mouth quirked upward in a cheeky grin.

"I shouldn't have asked," she said with a grimace. "Now, can we get to work?"

"Sure thing." He formed L shapes with his fingers to frame part of the open space with his hands. "I think the stage should go here. I was thinking of a square stage with a few lights hanging from the ceiling."

"Actually, I was thinking of something more unique." Autumn pointed down at the spot where she stood and moved her hand in a circular motion. "A round stage in the middle of the hall, with the guests sitting around it. It'll be the main focal point of the event while creating more room for tables and such."

"Ugh, that's a terrible idea. Interior designers and decorators will be flying in from all across the globe for this event. I'm sure they won't want to look at the back of someone's head while listening to presentations and watching their colleagues receive awards."

"Look, I know this space is massive, but I feel if we minimize a few things, we can add more to the project."

"Have you ever heard of 'less is more?'"

"I have, but I still think that adding a few inspired statement pieces and extra seating could be a better way to spice up the event."

"You know what, why don't we create a rendering of our

thoughts, and we'll pick and choose what we like from each?"

"That sounds like a good collaboration." She put her hands on her hips and looked around some more. "What were you thinking for the color scheme?"

"Stick with a simple palette. Royal blue, white, and silver." He glanced over at Autumn, who was unable to hide her disapproval. "Let me guess—you had different colors in mind."

"Hear me out. I was envisioning a more vibrant yet elegant theme with shades of crimson and gold. A pop of white sprinkled in throughout."

"That doesn't really fit this type of event, but you can put it in your 3D model render." He crossed his arms. "But ultimately, my mother will be having the final say."

Her shoulders sagged. "You're right. She'll probably change most of the project to fit her tastes."

"Well, for your ideas, probably. But she loves everything that I do."

"Of course she does," Autumn mumbled under her breath, turning away from the golden boy. Just wanting to get this over with, she asked, "Where should the food table go?"

"You haven't liked any of my ideas so far. So, where do *you* think it should go?"

She scanned the room quickly. "The wall at the back left. It's close to the club's kitchen area, so it'll be easy for both attendees and waiters to go back and forth."

Rodney nodded as he looked the area in question over. "I think for once we agree on something."

"Good." Autumn peeked at her watch. "Anything else

that's critical to address?"

"No, the rest is just filler." Rodney's eyes burned into Autumn as he asked, "Do you have a hot date or something?"

"No, but I do have other work I need to get finished. Plus, the sooner we leave here, the faster I can start on my 3D model and illustrations for the event."

"I guess we have seen all that we could at this venue. And we have a general idea on what we want to do with the space." Rodney fished out his phone from his front pocket and said, "We'll reconvene on Monday in my mother's office and get her final opinion on the design for the party setup and décor."

"That's fine. I should be able to scrap my portfolio together by then."

"I'll see you Monday, then. Have a good weekend, Autumn."

Reluctantly, she replied, "You too, Rodney."

With that she hurried off, eager to start mapping out her vision for the banquet hall. She wasn't sure whether Mrs. Lamour was going to like any of her ideas, especially since this event would put their agency in the national spotlight. All Autumn wanted was her moment to shine in this industry, and this would be the best chance to do it. If she could get even part of her vision showcased at the event, maybe she'd have a chance to move up in the interior decorating world.

July 8th

Autumn was running late, but she wasn't the only one. Mrs. Lamour was nowhere in sight. The only person in the boss' office when Autumn arrived was Rodney, who was rifling through papers on his mother's desk.

"Do you touch everyone's stuff when they're not looking?" Autumn asked as she wandered over with her sketches in hand.

Rodney turned halfway to her, a smug grin on his clean-shaven face. "Not everyone's. And anyway, it's only to get inspiration and ideas."

"Stealing, you mean."

He scowled. "No, expanding on original ideas and making them better."

"However you want to spin it to make yourself feel better."

"It's not spinning if it's the truth." His eyes fell to the papers she had clutched against her chest with her left arm. "Are those your proposed plans for the event?"

Her gaze went down to the papers as she answered, "Most of them. The good ones, anyway."

He reached out a hand for them and said, "Let me take a look at what you came up with."

She held the papers closer. "I think I'll wait until your mother arrives."

"It's not like I can steal it. We've already created what we wanted to show her." He grabbed the papers he'd been sifting through on his mother's desk and showed them to Autumn. "Here, you can look at mine while I look at yours."

With a resigned sigh, she handed over her work and took Rodney's from his outstretched hand. She flicked through his work as he did hers, and in doing so, she tried not to scoff at his mundane and boring designs. Ideas that had been done countless times and were wearing themselves out. Even the trendier plans were still lacking, and if she didn't already know that he enjoyed special treatment, she surely would have realized it now. There was no way he'd make it in the industry if it wasn't for his mother.

The click-clack of heels signaled someone walking into the room, and soon, Mrs. Lamour's voice followed. "Oh good, you two are here. My seven o'clock meeting ran a little late, but I'm eager to see what you two came up with."

"I'm sure you won't be disappointed, mother," Rodney said with a toothy smile.

Autumn moved to switch back her papers with Rodney, but in the shuffle, she bumped into his hands and knocked both sets of sketches and models onto the floor. Rodney snickered and said, "Nice going, clumsy."

She spared him a glare as she dropped down to retrieve the fallen papers. He bent down to help, scooping up whatever was his and handing over what was hers. It didn't take long before all the pictures were off the ground, and the two were sitting in the office chairs across from Mrs. Lamour.

"Are you both ready to present your ideas, or do you need more time?" she asked in a haughty tone, her expression peeved.

Autumn shook her head, still a bit flustered after the little mishap. "No, I'm ready to show you what I have."

Mrs. Lamour reached her manicured hand out for Autumn's work. She hastily handed the papers to her boss, crossing her fingers that her ideas would be good enough for the event. Mrs. Lamour lowered her black cat-eye glasses down from atop her head and onto the bridge of her nose as she studied every sheet of paper. She nodded as she continued to thumb through Autumn's rough sketches.

"Not bad," she mentioned as she splayed them down on her desk. "I like that you went with a more modern style, along with a gold-and-red theme. I also adore your idea of having miniature décor models to showcase people's works and highlight what we all do for a living. We may just have to work those into the project."

Before Mrs. Lamour could praise her ideas any further, Rodney thrust his stack of papers toward his mother, who shot him a bright smile as she took them. She flicked through his faster than Autumn's but soon stopped on one in particular. She laid it down and let out a short gasp, her mouth partially agape. "This is magnificent. I love the use of a round stage, and you have a similar color scheme to Autumn's as well."

Autumn quickly glanced at the paper on Mrs. Lamour's desk, realizing that her work had somehow gotten mixed up in his during the shuffle. Before she could claim it as hers, Rodney jumped in. "I thought it'd be cool to have something different and add more unique flair to the banquet. You know, instead of doing the same old thing as the previous years."

Autumn gaped at Rodney. She couldn't believe what she was hearing. Actually, she could. She knew he was famous for this kind of thing; she just didn't expect to be experiencing it firsthand. And worst of all, she couldn't even say anything because she'd forgotten to include her signature on that piece. She was livid, and not just at Rodney for not correcting his mother about the design's true owner. She was angry at herself for forgetting such a simple detail that she almost always included with her work. But she had been flying through her designs for the past week, not to mention her other decorating projects. With everything she was juggling she was bound to miss something. She just wished it hadn't been this.

"I think we'll go with this design right here. We'll also add some elements from Autumn's ideas, especially the cute little models." She clasped her hands together, the movement making her bracelet-clad arms jingle. "I knew I could count on you two to design this. I want you both to jump on the phone and computer so we can start ordering everything we need for the banquet."

"Yes, mother. We'll get right on it. Right, Autumn?" He glanced at her, and she fought to keep her cool in front of her boss.

With a curt nod and tight lips, she said, "Yes, we'll start getting everything in order."

"Great. I'll talk with you two soon," Mrs. Lamour said, dismissing them as she handed back their respective stacks.

The two left Mrs. Lamour's office and retreated toward their offices. Halfway down the hall, Autumn turned to face Rodney, her cheeks hot with rage and her heart pounding. She didn't like conflict, but she felt that this warranted a strong reaction. "How could you claim it as yours? You didn't even like that idea."

Rodney cocked his head to the side as he looked down

at her with a wry smirk. "It grew on me, and I took into consideration what you said. We should liven up the event this year and make it more unique."

"That's fine, but the least you could have done was tell your mother it was my idea, or even given me partial credit since it was my drawing."

"I mean, it was in my pile and there was no signature, so it could have been anyone's."

"So I forgot to sign it this one time. But it clearly looks like all of my previous work. It should have been obvious."

He shrugged his right shoulder. "Well, it's settled now. Plus, since I'm technically your other boss, all your ideas are also my ideas. We give and take from each other, especially in this line of work. We can create great things by putting our minds together and combining our thoughts and ideas."

"Sure, I can agree with *part* of that statement," she hissed as she crossed her arms in front of her. "But when one person is doing all of the taking and none of the giving, then that's not great teamwork. It's not even ethical."

He gave her a look that she couldn't quite read. "Then let me make it up to you."

"By waltzing back into your mother's office and telling her it was all my idea?"

"No . . . I was thinking about you being my date to the banquet. I'll introduce you to some of the big names you've only heard and read about in designer magazines."

She scoffed. "I don't see how being your date is making it up to me."

"Don't think of it as an actual date. We're both attending

anyway. Consider it an opportunity to schmooze with some big names in the industry and learn from them."

"I could do that myself."

"You could, but I know all these people—most of them since I was a kid. It'd be easier to strike up conversations with me as your in."

Autumn grunted in response as she mulled over what he was saying. She detested the idea of being his date, but he was right about one thing. Sticking with him would give her the chance to mingle with some prolific designers since she wasn't big in the business herself quite yet. Wringing her hands together as her stomach did somersaults, she said, "Fine, I'll attend the banquet with you, but not as a date. As long as you introduce me to some big names."

Rodney reached his hand out, a delighted smile creeping onto his face. "It's a deal."

Autumn shook his outstretched hand with reluctance, but the way she saw it, she didn't have much of a choice. At least this way, she was getting a little something out of her work being stolen. They parted ways in the corridor, and Autumn went back to her office. She doubted she'd be able to focus for the rest of the workday, but she pushed the deal out of her mind as she booked the items they needed for the event. She'd have time to vent about it later, hopefully to Elliot, if he had the time. But Levi would do just as well.

July 27th

"Wow! This place looks amazing," Autumn said, gawking at a couple of workers carrying out the last of the decorations for the banquet.

"It sure does, all thanks to my keen eye for design," Rodney said as he sidled up next to her in his elegant black tuxedo and turquoise tie that matched her dress.

"You mean *my* design?"

"Nuance. But it did turn out to be an astonishing display."

Autumn picked at the ruffled hip of her gown with a frustrated sigh. "I still can't believe I agreed to accompany you for the night."

"Me neither, but I'm glad you did. You look truly exquisite in that tight dress," he said as he gave her a once-over.

Feeling uncomfortable under his ogling stare, she crossed her arms in front of her body. She was grateful when their conversation was cut short as Mrs. Lamour sashayed toward them. "Oh, this is absolutely divine. Your visions came together beautifully. Especially the round stage in the center and the red-and-gold color scheme. I hope everyone else enjoys it as much as I do."

Rodney chuckled as he wrapped an arm around his mother's shoulder. "We'll find out soon enough. They should be letting guests inside within the next half hour."

"Wonderful." Mrs. Lamour turned to Autumn and said, "Thank you for being a part of this project. You two always work so well together."

She smiled at her boss and graciously replied, "I'm glad I could be a part of this special event. It's always been a dream to attend."

"Well, I hope you have fun tonight." The woman stole a glance at the thin gold watch around her wrist and said, "I have a few more things to do before everyone arrives. I'll see you two later at the banquet."

With a giddy shimmy of the shoulders, Mrs. Lamour was off to take care of her last-minute duties. Rodney turned to Autumn and said, "I'm going to keep an eye on the decorators and make sure they're putting everything in its rightful place. See you at the party, my lovely date."

He gave her a wink, which made her shudder internally. And not in a good way. With that, he sauntered off toward the back half of the room where a couple of workers were setting up one of the last model display pieces. Wanting to do her part, Autumn went to the back to give the workers a hand. So far, everything was going as planned, but the opinions of the prestigious guests were her main concern, the fear of their judgement lingering in the back of her mind.

As guests flooded the room and began to mingle, Autumn observed the party from afar. She watched as well-known designers and decorators chatted in small groups while waiting for the main event to begin. She wanted to greet everyone and pick their brains, but her body had other ideas. It was as though she couldn't physically step any closer to the party. Her nerves were getting the better of her as all the greats she'd only read about in magazines and newspapers stood right in front of her.

As she tried to bring herself to join the festivities, her

phone buzzed in her clutch. Fishing it out, she noticed a new text from Elliot. She opened the message. *"Hope I'm not bothering you. I just wanted to know how the party is going."*

She typed a short response back. *"Not too bad from what I can tell. Though the wallflower in me won't let me mingle."*

She didn't have to wait long for his reply. *"I'd probably be nervous at a function like that too. Just try to relax and have fun. And don't let that Rodney guy get to you."*

"I won't. I'll try to make this night one to remember. Talk to you later."

"Is that your boyfriend?" Rodney asked from beside her, not even hiding that he was peering over her shoulder at her phone. "Why didn't you invite him?"

Autumn shoved her phone back into her purse and glowered at Rodney. "Is nothing private to you?"

"I was just wondering what my date was up to."

"First of all, we agreed I'm not your date. Second, my personal conversations are none of your business."

From his smug expression, he seemed to be enjoying her flustered reaction. "It was a simple question. I was just wondering why a guy would miss out on seeing his girl in a delectable dress."

"He lives in Vermont. And he's just a friend I met a couple of years ago."

He raised his eyebrows. "Good to know."

She growled, "Look, just because I'm single doesn't mean you still have a chance. I want nothing to do with you, especially since you took my idea and passed it off as your own."

Rodney shrugged, a slight frown pulling at his thin lips.

"That's how the game is played. Sometimes you're bound to get stiffed. But if you truly want nothing to do with me, then our little arrangement is off. I thought you may have liked to be introduced to some of the best in the business, but I guess I was wrong."

Now it was Autumn's turn to frown. As much as she despised being near Rodney, missing out on an opportunity like this would be heartbreaking. Plus, whoever she met tonight could be her ticket out of Mrs. Lamour's office and into an even better one. "Wait . . . I did agree that I'd join you for the night. I'm not one to back out on my word, so I'll suck up my distaste for you and do as I promised."

Rodney gave her a knowing smirk as he wrapped an arm around her waist. "I knew you'd come to your senses."

Autumn didn't respond, already regretting her decision. She just hoped it would be worth it in the end.

Rodney breezed by several groups of people, briefly introducing Autumn. Many of them complimented the unique style of the event and were eager to see how the rest of the banquet played out with the round stage as the focal point. Autumn could barely get a word in to each guest as she was whisked away by Rodney to meet the next set of people. After a half hour, she was done being dragged around and decided to confront him during a lull in their endeavors.

"What are you doing?" Autumn hissed in a hushed whisper, her hands on her hips.

"Introducing you to everyone like I promised I'd do," he answered nonchalantly.

"I could hardly even shake hands with everyone with how fast we were breezing through. That's not what I had in mind when I signed up for this."

"How else would we get through all of these introductions in one night if we don't hop from one table to another? Good luck doing that if you're blabbering everyone's ears off."

"It's just simple conversation. I don't think the people you 'introduced' me to even knew I was there."

"Listen, I don't know what you want from me. I did what I agreed to do, and if you don't want to continue, then fine. Go mingle by yourself."

"Fine, I will." She looked around and said, "The banquet is about to start anyway, so I'll head to our table."

"Suit yourself," Rodney grumbled with a deadly glint in his eye before he shuffled off through the crowd.

Autumn sucked in a quick breath, trying not to let Rodney's antics ruin a day that should have been fun and exciting. She weaved her way through guests, too nervous to approach them, even though she really wanted to. Eventually, she reached the table where she, Mrs. Lamour, and Rodney were seated for the event, and her eyes roamed the room for someone to talk to. She didn't have to wait long when a tall and heavyset older man leaned over to her and asked in a deep tone, "Men trouble?"

She focused on the man next to her, realizing he wasn't just a nosy guest, but a multimillionaire with several interior decorating businesses stationed around the globe. Autumn pulled herself together, though she was still starstruck, and said, "Something like that. More like co-worker slash boss trouble."

"You work with Rodney Lamour, meaning you work under Margarete Lamour."

She nodded. "That would be correct."

The magnate gestured around the room. "Did you have a hand in all this?"

"I did, actually."

"I'm sure this was most of your doing."

Autumn gave him a suspicious look and said, "I . . . Kind of."

He chuckled. "I doubt Rodney could come up with something this stunning—and creative." The man paused and reached out a hand. "My name is Sal Cardoza, by the way."

She shook the man's plump hand and introduced herself. "I'm Autumn Burke, and I'm quite a fan of your work."

His eyes twinkled. "Thank you. I'm a fan of yours as well."

She blushed, feeling a rush of pride that her work was being recognized by a big name. Though she appreciated the praise, she was still curious how he knew Rodney wasn't heavily involved in the final design. So, she asked, "How did you know this wasn't Rodney's doing?"

He scoffed as his eyebrows knitted together. "A few years ago, I collaborated with Margarete on an Italian villa in Italy. I asked her to send out her best employee to work with my people, and she sent her son. Now, I wasn't fully involved in the project, but I got a lot of complaints from my people about the arrogant young man who wasn't too keen on working with others."

"Sounds about right."

"He tried using teammates' ideas, and even stealing some outdated versions of other respectable designers' previous works. I was appalled, but when I tried to bring it up with Margarete, I was promptly dismissed. Haven't worked with her since."

"Wow, that's a shame. I would have loved to be on a job like that."

"I'm sure you would have done a much better job, even as an amateur designer."

She cleared her throat, her face warm from the compliment. "I haven't heard much from your company as of late. Have you been cutting back on designing?"

"No, my company and businesses continue to expand every day. We just don't get much headliner work these days. Though I am planning on branching out to two new locations next year. That should put my company back on the map for a while."

Autumn offered him a genuine smile. "That's great to hear. Do you mind me asking where?"

"Not at all," he said, shaking his head with a hearty laugh. "I will have a smaller office in Vermont. Even though my main branch is in New York, I think that having a greater presence on the East Coast will do us well. I'm also looking at the Middle East or Asia for a branch. We have three spots in mind—Dubai, Mumbai, or Tokyo. But we haven't settled on one quite yet."

"My sister lives in Vermont actually, and I have a friend there. It seems like a nice state."

"Yes, it's quite lovely, especially during the wintertime.

My wife is from Vermont, so we used to take our girls there all the time for skiing and visiting family." Mr. Cardoza reached into his suit pocket, pulling out a matte cream card with gold lettering. Handing it to Autumn, he said, "If you ever want to collaborate or work under a different company, give me a call. Based on my experience tonight, I believe you might be a great fit."

Mixed emotions fluttered in her stomach as she politely replied, "Thank you for this, but I think I'm content where I am right now."

"Fair enough. But if you ever change your mind, I'm just a ring away." He gave her a small nod and a toothy grin before strutting away.

As Autumn sat down on the stool by her table, she looked over the fancy business card. She had already put in so much time and effort at Mrs. Lamour's Decorating company. It would be silly of her to move out East and start from the bottom again, wouldn't it? Sure, she'd be closer to Jillian—and of course, Elliot—but uprooting her whole life and leaving the state she'd called home since she was born? That was not in her plans.

Not that plans didn't change. She just wasn't sure if a big move was the best decision during this time of her life. Before she could delve deeper into her thoughts, the lights began to dim, signaling that the event was about to begin. Slipping the card into her purse so Mrs. Lamour or Rodney wouldn't see it, she got ready to finish the momentous evening with an entertaining show.

Chapter 15

Elliot

July 28th

Elliot struggled to haul a large cardboard box toward Angela's new living room. He lowered it onto the hardwood floor with a winded huff before taking a seat on top of it. While he wiped the sweat from his brow, Angela strolled through the open front door with a small box in hand. Plopping down next to him on the box, she released a long sigh. "I forgot how exhausting moving is."

"You moved three boxes in the last hour, and they weren't even that heavy," he retorted.

"But watching you lug some of these boxes was hard in itself. You know, sympathy pains."

"Sure, that's what it is. Not old age, since you're nearing

fifty."

Angela gasped, smacking Elliot's shoulder with the back of her hand. "Rude . . . But it's also true."

"You know I'm kidding." He chuckled, looking around the bare room half-filled with moving boxes. "I thought you got rid of most of your stuff from New York. How in the world did you accumulate all of this so fast?"

"Let's just say late-night QVC-watching and a few cups of wine aren't a good combination. At least everything I bought is useful, though."

"You sure about that, or is that what you tell yourself to feel better?"

She snickered and shook her head. "A bit of both. Seriously though, most are appliances that I would have needed for my new home anyway. I just got a head start."

"It's a nice place too; two beds and one-and-a-half baths. And for a good price. I'm happy for you."

Angela leaned into her brother as she said, "Thank you, Elliot. It's nothing compared to Mom and Dad's house, but I don't think I'll ever need that kind of space. You, on the other hand."

Elliot threw his hands out in front of him, palms facing forward. "Whoa, whoa. Let's not get ahead of ourselves. I'll be lucky if I ever fill up those three bedrooms, and I highly doubt that's going to happen. At least not anytime soon."

"You still have time to settle down. Plus, you've been chatting with that girl from Seattle, right?"

"Well, yeah, but that's all we're doing. Talking. Our friendship won't move beyond that, because she lives there and I live here. Autumn and I will never be together."

She rolled her eyes. "Whatever you say, little brother."

Before he could counter her statement, his phone rang. He checked the caller ID, feeling the presence of his sister leaning over to catch a glimpse of the name on the screen. When he saw it was Autumn, he heard his sister mumble, "Nothing serious . . ."

"It's just a phone call."

She gave him a knowing smile. "Go ahead and use the guest room. I'll bring in some more boxes." With that, she slid off the box and headed toward the front door.

"Okay, just don't hurt yourself."

"I make no promises."

Elliot retreated into the guest room, closed the door behind him, and picked up the call. "Hey, Autumn. What's up?"

"Nothing much. I just wanted to tell you how last night went," she replied in a chipper tone.

"Oh right, the banquet. Did Rodney give you a hard time?"

"Ugh, like always. He promised to introduce me to the talented people there, and he wound up doing it in the worst possible way. I barely even spoke with anyone because he was flying through them so fast."

Elliot felt a pang of annoyance. "You didn't take that crap from him, did you?"

"No. I confronted him right away, and he left me alone for the rest of the night. Which I was honestly grateful for."

"Besides that, did you have a good time?"

"Yes, it was wonderful," she gushed. "I even met one of

the biggest interior decorating CEOs from New York, Sal Cardoza, and he was so nice. He even gave me his card and practically offered me a job at his new branch."

Elliot felt himself smiling. "Wow, that's awesome. Are you going to take it?"

Her tone softened. "I don't know. I've been working at Mrs. Lamour's agency since my college internship, and I've been gradually moving up in the company over the last seven years. I couldn't possibly give it all up to move across the country and start from zero."

"Wait, moving across the country? Is the new branch in New York?" he asked, curious how close she could be to him if she took this new job.

"Actually, it's kind of funny. It would be in Vermont."

Elliot could have sworn his heart skipped a beat. Reminding himself to breathe, he stammered, "Oh, I wasn't expecting that."

"I was shocked too. I'd be much closer to my sister, and I could finally meet you in person. But like I said, it's just too big of a risk."

He stemmed his excitement. "You're right. It is a huge decision to make. I've been thinking about expanding my business and franchising it out, but I'm scared to make that jump."

"Business decisions are never easy, especially when your whole life and financial situation are tied to that decision."

"Exactly." He breathed out a sigh. "So, I don't blame you for being wary about jumping ship. And I'm sure you have some time to think about it."

"Thanks, I'll definitely be keeping it in mind. The

opportunity is still on the table, maybe not forever, but for a while."

"Whatever you choose, I wish you luck. Though, it would be cool to have you closer."

Her giggle rose on the other end as she said, "I'm sure you would, and honestly, so would I. Maybe someday."

"Maybe."

After a brief silence, Autumn changed the subject. "What are your plans today?"

Elliot looked around Angela's half-empty guest room and answered, "I've spent most of the day helping my sister move."

"Angela moved out? I know you told me you were helping her look for places, but I didn't know she found a spot. I bet you're going to miss her."

"It's been nice having her around, but I've also been missing my privacy just a bit. At least she's not as far as she used to be."

"I get it. I lived with my sister for a year before she moved in with her boyfriend, now husband. It was fun for a couple of months, but then it got old fast."

"Well, it was an experience."

Autumn sighed and said, "I don't want to keep you long. I have a lunch date with Levi in a couple of hours, so I should get ready."

"Have fun, and I'll talk to you again soon."

They said their goodbyes, and Elliot reluctantly ended the call before wandering out of the guest room. Angela was digging through one of the boxes stacked in her living room. Striding up next to her, he asked, "Need some help unpacking?"

"Nah, I got it from here," she replied as she spun around to face him. "You go spend the rest of your Sunday doing something fun."

"The only 'fun' thing on my usual Sunday agenda is painting at the rec' center."

"Then go and paint."

"I can skip a weekend. It's not like it cost me anything."

Angela put her hands on her hips and said, "I thought you liked it. Now you don't want to go?"

"I mean, it's relaxing, and it gets me out of the house for something other than work," he answered with a shrug. "I just hate being the center of attention. Most of the attendees are divorced older women, some would be around Mom's age if she were still alive. And they always fawn over me as soon as I step into the art room."

"Aww, I don't blame them. You're just so cute and lovable."

"Ange, please . . ." he grumbled, showing his displeasure with a scowl.

"Okay, okay." Angela picked up a toaster from her current box and handed it to Elliot. "Welp, if you don't want to get artsy today, then make yourself useful."

"I don't mind helping out," he said as he took the toaster into the small kitchen across the way.

"So, how's your girlfriend doing?"

"She's not my girlfriend, but she's doing fine. Got a new job offer."

Angela paused her rifling. "Oh, good for her, but I assume it's bad for you."

"Why bad for me?" he asked as he found a spot for the toaster on the countertop.

"If she keeps moving up in her line of work, there's no chance that you'd ever meet and have the chance to fall madly in love."

"The thing is, the job offer is for a new interior decorating hub here in Vermont."

"No way! Here?" Angela's face brightened as she practically bounced with excitement. "Then that's great news. Is she going to take it?"

Elliot shook his head, pushing down the feeling of despondence that threatened to bubble up. "No. She's content where she's at, and I don't blame her. If she took the position and it was mostly for us to be together, then if things didn't work out, she'd be stuck with a life filled with resentment and regrets."

"I see your point, but it could also work out for the both of you."

"It could, but who'd want to take that chance?"

She exhaled slowly. "Agreed. I wouldn't switch my life around for a man." Angela picked up another appliance from the box and said, "Why don't we work our way through these boxes and get some pizza for dinner?"

"As long as you're paying," he said as he opened up another box.

"You bet I am. Consider it my reward for your help."

He snickered. "I guess it's better than nothing."

They continued to unpack for the rest of the evening, getting most of the boxes emptied before dinner arrived. Elliot's mind lingered on Autumn's news. If he was being honest with himself, he wished that the job opportunity was good enough to make her take it. He'd tried to fool everyone around him, and even himself, into believing that he hadn't fallen for the woman, but it was a flat-out lie. He liked Autumn. A lot. Possibly even loved her, after all the conversations they'd shared. He just wanted her to be closer so he could explore whatever these feelings might be. Especially if they were mutual.

Chapter 16

Autumn

December 3rd

Autumn had been swamped with work since the party back in July. After hosting the banquet, the company was booming with new clients, being flooded with requests from all over Seattle and across Washington state. But she wasn't complaining about the sudden spike in popularity, especially since Mrs. Lamour had decided to up everyone's pay by ten percent.

Today, she was meeting with a new client at their luxurious log cabin tucked on the shoreline of a bay an hour outside of Seattle. As she waited for the couple on the dreary Tuesday morning, a frigid breeze numbing her face, a familiar Lamborghini drove up the long driveway.

Her mood plummeted as Rodney stepped out of the vehicle and strutted toward her. She didn't bother to hide her annoyance as she asked, "What are you doing here?"

"My mother asked if I could oversee this project. So, we're working together once again," he answered as he wrapped an arm around Autumn's shoulder. "Aren't you excited?"

She shrugged off his embrace. "No, I wanted to do this alone. Or with anyone except you."

"Harsh words. But you don't have a choice. You're stuck with me because my mother likes us together."

She fixed him in a glare. "Fine. Just don't take my ideas this time."

"Oh, come on. Last time, things just got a little mixed up and became a big misunderstanding. It shouldn't happen again."

As he spoke, a silver Lexus pulled up next to the other cars in the driveway, and the older couple hobbled out of the vehicle. Autumn cut her conversation short with Rodney and greeted their clients. "Hello, Mrs. and Mr. Fillan. I'm Autumn. I'll be one of the decorators for your home."

The couple strode right past Autumn and straight over to Rodney. Mrs. Fillan pulled him into a small hug, kissing each of his cheeks. "Oh, I'm so glad you're here. I asked your mom if you could be a part of this project, and I'm thrilled you could make it."

"I couldn't say no to you, Gwen," he said with a bright smile.

Mr. Fillan gripped Rodney's shoulder with his wrinkled hand and said, "My, have you grown since you played ball with Bobby!"

"I finally hit that growth spurt." He chuckled as he gestured toward his long legs. "How is Bobby, by the way?"

"Oh, he's great. Graduated from Harvard at the top of his class six years ago, became a lawyer in California, and just had a handsome baby boy with his wife."

Rodney's eyes widened. "Wow, a dad already?"

Mr. Fillan beamed. "Yep, how about you?"

"Not yet. I haven't found anyone to settle down with, but I'm sure it'll happen soon."

Mrs. Fillan flicked her wrist dismissively, clucking her tongue. "I'm sure you'll find the right girl. You're a lovely young man, Rodney."

Trying to tame her rising irritation, Autumn cleared her throat, hoping to get everyone's attention. All eyes landed on her as she said, "I hate to interrupt, but I think we should get to work."

"And who are you?" Mrs. Fillan asked in a haughty tone.

Before she could answer, Rodney interjected, "This is my coworker, Autumn. She'll be helping me with this project."

The older woman raised her eyebrows. "Is she any good?"

"She's been working for us for a while. Even planned the Interior Designing and Decorating banquet a few months ago with me."

"Okay, then. I trust you and your mother's judgment." Without sparing a glance at Autumn, she started toward the front entrance of the home and said, "Why don't we get started, shall we?"

When the four of them entered the cabin, Autumn noticed that it was pretty bare. They would have to furnish most of the place and figure out what style their clients wanted to achieve. As she surveyed the enormous living area and eyed the high vaulted ceilings, she asked, "Will this be your full-time home or your vacation home?"

Mr. Fillan was the one to answer. "Vacation home. We currently live in California to be close to our son and grandson."

Autumn continued, "Do you want to make it your home away from home or go with a more rustic feel? Maybe even a luxury style?"

"No, I don't want it to be luxurious," Mrs. Fillan said as she leaned against the spacious kitchen island. "I do like the idea of an antique look. How about you, Harvey?"

"Rustic is good," he answered. "I've always been a sucker for that old-fashioned style."

Rodney jumped in, "We can do that. Rustic happens to be my area of expertise as well."

Mrs. Fillan nodded approvingly. "Fantastic. We'll do the whole house in that style."

Autumn took out her phone, jotting down notes of what they were planning for the home. "How many rooms does this place have?"

"Three bedrooms, a den, plus the living room and kitchen we're standing in. Also, two and a half baths."

"We'll figure out some plans and a general idea of placements for the furniture."

"Yep," Rodney said as he meandered toward the den. "We'll get right on that once we check out the rest of the house."

It didn't take them long to complete a walkthrough of the rest of the cabin. As they moved from room to room, Autumn felt invisible. She hoped this project wouldn't be another instance of her hard work being overlooked because of Rodney.

December 10th

Autumn was frantically rummaging through her desk as she searched for one of the half-finished sketches of her concepts for the Fillan cabin. But she wasn't having much luck. She could have sworn she brought it in the other day to add a few finishing touches, and she was hoping to finish it before their meeting at four. Autumn took a minute to rerun the previous day in her head, trying to remember whether she brought it home with her. She didn't recall doing that, but there was always a possibility that she'd picked it up with some other papers as she got ready to go home. She quickly calculated how long it would take to run home and grab it, but if it was there, she didn't even know where it might have ended up. By the time she got back to work, she wouldn't have the time to complete the sketch to show the Fillans.

She decided to scrap that particular idea and went with her second choice, which was more complete. Hunching over her worktable, she finished up the last touches to the living room and den. But before she could get very far in her creative process, a knock sounded at her door. Autumn craned her neck to the entryway to see Rodney stepping inside. She groaned and asked, "What do you want? I'm busy finishing my sketch for the Fillan cabin."

"Then you better hurry because they'll be here soon," he responded, leaning over her desk.

She felt her breath hitch in her throat. "They're not supposed to be here until four."

"Well, they moved up the time of the meeting, so you got," —he checked the watch on his arm— "roughly twenty minutes."

"Twenty minutes! When did they move the meeting up?"

"About two hours ago. It completely slipped my mind until now, but I figured I should let you know."

"You forgot!" she snapped. Autumn shot out of her seat as she gathered her things for the meeting. "Something tells me that's a bunch of baloney. You did this to me on purpose."

"I didn't," Rodney defended as he watched Autumn flit around the room. "I lost track of time and realized they'd be here sooner than expected."

"Sure you did."

"Listen, it's not my fault you weren't prepared for the meeting today."

"Like *you're* ready . . . Do you even have anything for today?"

Rodney nodded, a smile teasing his lips. "Yes, I got a bit of inspiration last night and came up with something I think they might like."

"Well, I'll be ready for them." Autumn shooed him with her hand and said, "Can you leave so I can get my stuff in order?"

He took a step toward the door, shooting a cocky grin.

"I'll see you at the meeting, then."

Rodney left the room with a suspicious amount of pep in his step, but Autumn could care less. She needed to complete her finishing touches, and in a lot less time than she'd planned. She only hoped it would be enough to compete with Rodney's design, whatever that may be.

Autumn entered the meeting room only a few minutes late, but everyone was already gathered around the conference table. Mrs. Lamour, Rodney, and the Fillans were poring over what she assumed was Rodney's sketch. When she reached them and peered down at the photo, she audibly gasped at the sight. It was her design, the one she couldn't find from last evening, but with slight changes since it hadn't been complete. All eyes fell on her, and she didn't know what to say. Did she compliment the work that belonged to her and hand over the praise to a conniving thief? Or take the plunge and point out that his work was hers? She knew she probably wouldn't have much luck with the latter, so she forcefully mumbled through her teeth, "That's a nice layout and design."

"Isn't it, Autumn?" Mrs. Lamour gushed as she admired the drawing. "I think this may be one of your best works yet, Rodney."

"I think so too, mother," he replied with a self-satisfied tip of his chin. "I stayed up all night perfecting it."

Autumn grumbled under her breath, "Yeah, to change my idea just enough to pass it off as your own."

Mrs. Fillan gestured toward "Rodney's" picture and said,

"Honestly, I feel we don't even have to look at much more. This is stunning, and I'm sure if we can find the right pieces of décor, it'll really bring a pop of life to our little cabin."

"Are you positive that's what you want to go with? We can always change it, but that'll cost extra depending on how far we are into the process," Mrs. Lamour explained.

"I'm positive. Harvey, your thoughts?"

Mr. Fillan shrugged as he bit at his bottom lip. "It exudes good taste. I like the touch of western style thrown in too."

Rodney gave a manly chuckle and said, "I did that just for you, Harv. You always talked about John Wayne and Clint Eastwood movies back in the day."

The elderly man smiled and winked. "Ah, you got me there."

"I guess that settles it, then," Mrs. Lamour exclaimed. "We'll get everything ordered and ready to go. Hopefully, we'll have some items arriving soon after Christmas, and we'll start setting up your cabin."

"That sounds great," Mrs. Fillan said as she clasped her hands together. "I can't wait to spend our summer there with the family next year."

Mrs. Lamour responded with a graceful nod. "I'm sure it'll be lovely."

The Fillans left the room with Mrs. Lamour as they chatted about their future property. Autumn stayed back, snatching Rodney's upper arm and yanking him to face her. "How could you do this?"

"Do what?" he asked, a villainous smile spreading across his face. "I didn't do anything."

"You stole my sketch. It was in my office last night."

"Can you prove that?"

"I . . . No, I can't. But why? Why did you do it?"

His face hardened, a dangerous glimmer reaching his eyes. "No one turns me down and makes me look like a fool in front of hundreds of acquaintances." Rodney started picking up his things, but his gray-hued eyes never left hers. "I tried to be nice to you, Autumn, but you never reciprocated my generosity. So I'm going to use you every chance I get to help boost my career, one project at a time."

She gaped at him. "You're doing this because I won't sleep with you, or go on a date with you?"

He shrugged. "Pretty much."

"That's not fair," Autumn said as she tried to wrap her head around Rodney's manipulative knack. "I can get you fired for this."

He sneered. "I'd like to see you try. I doubt it'll go over the way you hope."

She set her jaw, planting her feet down as she fixed him in a hard stare. "I'm not scared of you."

Rodney ignored her, sauntering toward the door before turning back to glance at her. "Well, you should be, because it's your word against mine, and you know how that'll pan out. But hey, maybe I'll throw you a bone every once in a while if I think you deserve it."

With that, he was gone, and Autumn was left staring at the door, her breathing ragged. His sudden bluntness left her in shock. He wasn't even trying to hide his wrongdoings anymore, and she didn't know if that bothered her more than his constant denials. Feeling lost and helpless, Autumn dragged her feet back to her office. Levi must have noticed that something was wrong because he was beside her within seconds. As they walked the small corridor back to her office, he quietly asked, "What's wrong? What happened?"

"He stole my work again," is all she could muster.

"Again? That jerk. Did you confront him?"

"Of course, but he practically threw it in my face this time. He said he'll keep doing it, too, all because I won't date him."

"What a selfish pig." Levi stepped in front of Autumn, stopping her in her tracks. His expression was unyielding. "You have to tell her."

Her eyes flew wide. "No way! I can't get fired."

"Well, you can't keep getting your ideas stolen either."

Autumn glanced over her shoulders to make sure no one was eavesdropping. "I'll figure something out, but for now, I'll have to let Rodney do what he wants."

"You cannot let that man take advantage of you. You should be the one getting lofty praise and working at the highest level in the company, not him and your ideas."

"Levi, listen, I know you mean well, but I can't do that. Let me come to terms with this until I can come up with a more foolproof game plan."

His shoulders sagged as he relented, "Do whatever you need to, but I don't want to see you getting hurt anymore. I won't interfere, but I think my time here at the company is coming to an end."

Autumn could only blink back in surprise, her breath catching in her lungs. "What?"

"I can't stand by and watch my friend get stepped on,

over and over, by the boss and her son. I think I'll be turning in my resignation soon."

Autumn's chest tightened at the thought of her closest friend leaving. "Levi, are you sure? You're going to quit, just like that?"

"You best believe it. I don't need a plan. I know things will turn out fine for me." He shrugged with surprising nonchalance. "Plus, I've recently been looking at some fashion design courses in California. But I didn't want to leave my best friend behind, so I opted to stay here."

"I didn't realize you were thinking about switching careers." Autumn shook her head in disbelief as she stared down at the tiled floor. "I've been a terrible friend."

He rushed forward, placing a reassuring hand on her shoulder. "No, you haven't. You've been the best friend anyone could ask for. You've just been preoccupied with a certain handsome fella in Vermont and tormented by a dastardly coward here in Seattle."

"Maybe . . . maybe I *should* think about leaving. I can't let him do this to me anymore."

Levi gave her a soft smile. "Whatever you decide, I'll be here for you. I promise."

"Thank you, Levi." She wrapped her arms around his waist and stole a much-needed hug.

He patted her back and said, "You're welcome."

After a long embrace, Autumn pulled away, wiping off a few stray tears that had escaped. "Well, I'm going to get back to work—and start thinking about my final decision."

"And I'm going to settle *my* final decision by writing up that resignation letter and applying to that school I've been dying to attend."

They went their separate ways, and Autumn slipped into her office with a heavy heart and full mind as she contemplated her next move. As she mulled over her future, she pulled out the card she had received from Mr. Cardoza five months ago, wondering whether this was the push that she needed to make the jump to a new job . . . and a new state.

With her brain working out every potential scenario, she decided to call Elliot to get his thoughts on her situation. She already knew his opinion would be that she should take the job in Vermont. He'd clearly do anything to have her closer to him so they could meet in person, and she had to admit that she wanted the same thing. But her nerves always got the best of her when her thoughts drifted in that direction. She hated not knowing whether what they had was real and not just some fantasy they'd dreamed up over the phone.

After only a few rings, Elliot picked up her FaceTime call. She noticed that he was on his couch, his dress shirt unbuttoned at the top to reveal, some of his chest, a region of his body she'd never seen before.

"Hi, Elliot. How are you?" She asked, trying not to stare at the exposed skin peeking from under his shirt.

"I'm good. How are you? You look kind of sad," he asked, scrutinizing her with a furrowed brow from the other end.

She forced a chuckle. "You noticed?"

"Of course. I've gotten to know you well enough to sense when something is wrong."

She sucked in a breath, mentally preparing herself. "You

remember Rodney, right?"

Elliot straightened up, his nostrils flaring as irritation flashed across his face. "What did he do this time?"

"He stole the sketch I was working on for our current project. I knew I had left it in my office overnight, but I didn't think he'd grab it from my desk while I was gone."

"He stole another idea from you? He's lucky I live across the country, because that guy deserves a strong talking to. Or maybe something more."

"I appreciate you looking out for me, but it's fine."

"No, it's not fine," he snapped, his volume rising. "This guy is awful to you, and I don't know why you put up with him."

"It's not that easy." Autumn sighed, tilting her head back until she could see the ceiling of her office. "Like I told Levi, I can't just quit and leave. I've worked so hard, made it so far."

His tone softened. "I get that, but it doesn't seem like they're noticing you anymore. You'll be left behind while he gets all your credit, and then others will surpass you. And that doesn't sound like something you signed up for."

"You're right. But I'm scared I'll make the wrong decision and be stuck as a rookie decorator for the rest of my life."

"Well, think of it this way. Would you rather be stuck in your current position with a guy who treats you like dirt and takes everything you've done from you?"

"No, I guess not." Autumn hung her head, a wave of despair washing over her. "I just don't know what to do."

"No one ever does, but we all have to make tough

decisions at some point in our life. But doing nothing isn't an option anymore, from what I can tell."

"To be honest, I was thinking about that job offer in Vermont, but I don't know if I'm ready for such a big change."

"I understand completely." Elliot leaned back on the couch, his blue eyes brimming with compassion. "I can't tell you what to do, but I think it's time for you to look at better options, including the offer in Vermont. Who knows? Maybe that's where you were meant to be all along."

A small smile crept onto her face, and she said, "Maybe it is."

They continued to chat for another hour. Autumn was relieved when the conversation moved on to lighter subjects. But her mind still wandered to Rodney's conniving ways and her imperiled job, forcing her to ask herself whether it was finally time to say goodbye and move on from this stage of her life.

Chapter 17

Elliot

December 11th

Elliot paced his office floor as he aggressively typed on his phone's keyboard. He'd taken his lunch break to look up information on Autumn's workplace, indignant that her hard work and ideas continued to go unnoticed. He knew he really shouldn't be meddling in her business, but if she wasn't going to stand up for herself, then he would. Elliot found the number to her agency and loaded it onto his phone. His thumb circled the call button, his palms sweating. There was no turning back once he called. Without another thought, Elliot pressed the call button and stilled himself as it rang. Before long, someone answered. "Lamour's Interior Design Company. This is

Jenny. How can I help you today?"

"Hello, may I speak with Mrs. Lamour, please?" Elliot asked the woman.

"Can I ask who's calling?"

"This is . . ." Elliot hesitated as he thought of what to say. He figured he shouldn't use his real name, so he went with an alias. "I'm Eli Newton."

"You're not listed in our system. May I ask what this call is about?"

He cleared his throat. "I was looking to redo part of my home."

"You'd like to use our services for your upcoming project?"

"Yes, I would."

He heard a few clicks on the other end. "Okay. I just checked, and Mrs. Lamour is available to speak with you at the moment. Would you like me to patch you through?"

"Please."

"I'll forward your call then. Have a good day, Mr. Newton."

Before he could thank the woman, the soft jazz notes of a holding tune began to play. With every piano riff, his nerves mounted. Elliot tugged at the loose collar of his gray t-shirt, heaving a few breaths to calm himself.

"Lamour's Interior Design Company. This is Margarete Lamour speaking," Autumn's boss announced in a confident voice on the other end.

"Hello, Mrs. Lamour. I'd like to discuss something," Elliot said as pleasantly as he could.

"Are you looking to have one of my team members

decorate for you?"

"Not exactly. I'd like to discuss the way you've treated some of your employees."

Her tone took a sharp turn. "Excuse me! I don't know who you are, but I treat all my employees equally and fairly."

"As fair as you treat your son, Rodney?"

"Rodney gets no special treatment from me," she said, her voice laced with indignance.

"Doesn't he? I've heard that he steals from fellow workers and if anyone happens to confront him and call him out, they're the ones to face the repercussions."

Her voice lowered to a deadly rumble. "Listen, sir, you have some nerve calling my office and wasting my precious time with this nonsense."

"I just wanted to bring your attention to a situation that's hurting your employees. It also doesn't help that your son makes advances on women in the workplace when they clearly aren't interested."

"Have a good day," Mrs. Lamour said in an exasperated manner.

The phone clicked before silence took over. He stuffed his phone into his back pocket and let out a groan. That was a disaster. Shuffling out to the main area of the café, he felt a lot less like a knight in shining armor and more like pond scum after this monumental failure. Astrid stepped up to him with one of their only white hand towels thrown over her shoulder and asked, "What's wrong?"

"What do you mean?" Elliot asked, trying to act casual. "There's nothing wrong."

"You have that look like a child who's done something they shouldn't have and knows they're in trouble."

He sighed, his eyes falling to the floor. "I called Autumn's office and spoke with her boss."

Astrid's jaw dropped. "Oh sweetie, you didn't."

Elliot leaned against the front counter, resting his elbows on the glossy marble surface as he dragged a hand down his face. "I did."

Astrid shook her head with a sympathetic look. "Well, what did you say to her boss?"

He explained the whole situation and then tacked on, "But I never mentioned Autumn's name or my own. So, she shouldn't get into any trouble."

"You better hope they don't link it back to her," Astrid scolded. "She'd never forgive you for getting her fired from what otherwise sounds like her dream job."

"I know." He drew in a deep breath and exhaled slowly. "I don't even know why I'm worried that I might have just messed up my chances with her. It's not like I've ever really had a shot anyway."

"If that's how you feel. But it seems like you two were getting pretty close."

He let out a bitter chuckle. "Sure. As close as you can get when you're exchanging a handful of phone calls throughout the year. It's just a fun little friendship. That's all it'll ever be."

She joined him in leaning against the counter. "Well, whatever may or may not happen with this, I would tell her what you've done, just in case it does come back to you or her. That way she won't be caught off guard—and maybe just maybe—she won't be as mad at you for ruining her life."

"I guess I could do that."

Dragging himself out of his self-pity, Elliot decided to get back to work, even if it was another slow day. As he watched Astrid unpack another bag of paper coffee cups, Elliot tried to decide how he would break the news to Autumn about his big meddling mistake. More than likely, he'd just put her job in jeopardy, and he doubted she'd take that information well. Was it really the right thing to tell her, or should he just keep it to himself?

Elliot could barely eat his supper, which consisted of a lone bowl of chicken-flavored ramen. His stomach was in knots as he flip-flopped back and forth on what to do. As time ticked by, slowly approaching the time he'd be able to call her on the West Coast, Elliot's heart was pounding in his chest. He took out his cell phone, trying to decide between a regular phone call or a FaceTime call. He decided on a FaceTime call. That had been their norm as of late, and he didn't want to seem suspicious right off the bat. He just hoped his face didn't give anything away.

Autumn answered quicker than he expected. But all he could see was a blur of her clothing and what looked to be her kitchen in the background. Soon, all Elliot saw was the white ceiling with a small portion of a flat lighting fixture. Confused, Elliot asked, "Are you okay, Autumn? Did I catch you at a bad time?"

Autumn's frazzled face popped onto the screen. "No . . . kind of. Maybe you can help me?"

"With what?"

She picked up her phone, switching the camera view to the back-facing camera. Elliot was now staring into a pot of sludge. The concoction was gray with specs of black that looked a lot like scorched morsels. He couldn't even tell what the pot's contents were supposed to be, nor the consistency.

"What am I looking at?" he asked.

"A rice recipe that I wanted to try out." She flipped the camera back to her flustered face as she explained, "You see, I got some microwavable egg rolls, so I thought I'd make rice to go with it. Instead of doing my usual white rice with butter, I thought I'd find something new on the internet. Twenty-five minutes later, I'm left with this." She gestured to where the mystery pot still simmered.

"That's not rice . . . You've created a whole new entity." He snickered. "Has it tried to communicate with you?"

The corners of her lips pulled down. "Not funny, Elliot."

"Okay, in all seriousness, there is no saving that concoction."

"I know that I can't save it. I'm not even going to try to eat this disaster. I just want to know if I can save this pot. My grandmother gave it to me, and I don't want to throw it out."

"Hmm . . ." Elliot thought for a moment. "Maybe you can clean out what you can. Then, add water to the pot along with some dish soap. After an hour of soaking, try using a crumpled sheet of aluminum foil to scrub off the burnt food. I also heard that soap, water, and a dryer sheet, or fabric softener, could loosen the caked-on stuff."

Her expression morphed from irritation to surprise.

"Where'd you learn this?"

"I took a few culinary classes, mostly in high school, but a couple in college too. Our teacher—eccentric but good at his job—gave us some tips and tricks for cleaning our dishes. I'm not sure how well they'll work, but it's worth a try."

"Thanks, Elliot. I'll try one or two of those tricks on my pot. I really don't want to be the one to ruin my grandmother's cook ware."

"No problem. Let me know how it works."

"Will do." Autumn started filling up the pan with water and asked, "What did you call about? I kind of bombarded you with my situation."

Elliot bit his bottom lip and tried to sound casual. "Nothing in particular. I was just wondering how your day went."

"It was fine. I worked on some illustrations and 3D renderings of a few room concepts I had in mind for my latest clients."

"That's great. Nothing, uh, out of the ordinary happened at work?"

Autumn's eyebrows scrunched together in obvious confusion, "No, why?"

"No reason. I just know you were having some issues with that guy . . . Rodney, right?"

"Oh . . ." She shook her head. "Nothing has happened with him as of late. He seems to be keeping to himself, which I'm grateful for."

Elliot smiled, but the guilt weighing on his chest was starting to make him nauseous. He pushed the feeling down and said, "I hope his good behavior continues for you."

"Thank you. So do I."

"Well, I'll let you get back to cleaning your monstrosity."

Autumn let out a snort of laughter "Gee, thanks."

"You're welcome. See you later."

"Yeah, we'll chat soon!"

After ending the FaceTime call, Elliot rubbed his hand up and down his right cheek, his three-day-old stubble brushing against his fingertips. Part of him felt ridiculous for not telling her the truth, but the other part hoped she'd never find out. If that was the case, there was nothing for him to fret about. But if his interference did come out, who knew what reactions Autumn would throw back at him? One thing was for sure—they wouldn't be good.

Chapter 18

Autumn

December 12th

Autumn clicked through the 3D renderings, scrutinizing each concept. Her current clients were redoing the whole downstairs section of their house, so she had to make sure their living room, den, and kitchen fit the aesthetic they were trying to achieve. As she was zooming in on one of the renderings, a short knock sounded on her half-closed office door. She glanced up to see the receptionist and assistant to Mrs. Lamour, Jenny, who was only a couple of years younger than Autumn. The petite woman stepped into the room as she wrung her hands together. "Ms. Burke, Mrs. Lamour would like to see you in her office."

Autumn gave the nervous woman a comforting smile

and asked, "Did she say why?"

Jenny swallowed hard. "I think you want to hear it from her."

Autumn stood from her seat, confused. Why would Mrs. Lamour want to see her out of the blue like this? She followed Jenny back to Mrs. Lamour's office, breaking away when Jenny took a seat at the reception desk. Autumn walked into her boss's office to find both Mrs. Lamour and Rodney waiting for her. Her confusion only increased as she looked back and forth between them. Maybe it had something to do with the Fillan cabin?

Mrs. Lamour gestured to one of the leather chairs in front of her desk, and Autumn complied with the silent demand. Once she was seated, Mrs. Lamour folded her hands, intertwining her thin fingers and resting them on her uncluttered desk. "Do you know why I called you in here, Ms. Burke?"

Autumn shook her head. "I'm not sure. No."

"Yesterday morning, I received a call, thinking it was a prospective client. But no, this man instead berated me and accused me of nepotism."

"That's awful . . . But what does that have to do with me?"

She cocked her head slightly, fixing Autumn in a cold stare. "After that infuriating phone call, I had Jenny look into where the call came from. She tracked down the area code and found that it was located in Vermont." Mrs. Lamour gestured to Rodney, who was standing beside her. "Rodney overheard my conversation with Jenny and informed me that you had a male friend who lives there."

Rodney nodded, his arms crossed defiantly. "Yes, I

remembered you talking about some guy named Elliot at the banquet, and you mentioned that he lived in Vermont. It's also no secret that you strongly dislike me."

Autumn could only sit back in shock as she listened to their accusations. "There are at least five hundred thousand people who live in Vermont. How can you possibly be sure it was him?"

"It makes sense. Who else would know enough about this place to make those outrageous claims besides someone who's been told about it? I'm sure you've vented to that man about your job at least a few times."

She raised her hands and relented, "Okay, sure, I have told Elliot about my time here and the stress I was feeling. But he would never go behind my back like that." Autumn let out a solemn sigh and mumbled to herself, "He wouldn't break my trust like that."

Mrs. Lamour chimed in, "Whether this fellow was your acquaintance or not, I think it's best if we let you go."

"Let me go!" Autumn echoed, her mouth agape and her eyes flying wide. "You're going to fire me for something that might have nothing to do with me?"

Mrs. Lamour leaned forward, her face filled with pity. "I'm sorry, Autumn. You were a great asset to the company, and truly talented. I just can't have someone here who could tarnish my business, accusing me of things I didn't do."

Autumn's mouth went dry. "That's it? Just like that . . ."

Rodney shrugged, shoving his hands into his pockets. "Sometimes that's how it is. But we'll put in a good word for you somewhere else, promise."

Mrs. Lamour nodded in agreement, oblivious to

Rodney's face of pure delight as he helped put Autumn's career to an end. "Whatever you may find out there, don't hesitate to list us as a reference. Good luck out there, Ms. Burke."

Autumn stumbled up from the chair, still feeling dumbstruck as she dragged herself out of Mrs. Lamour's office. She couldn't process anything, her stomach rolling as she staggered back to her office. Once there, all she could do was stare down at her desk overflowing with unfinished work. She didn't even know where to begin. After all, cleaning her desk hadn't been on her to-do list today. Levi shuffled in without a knock since she'd left her door wide open. His face twisted in confusion, but a trace of compassion was laced into his expression. Walking up to the front of her desk, he asked, "What's Wrong? Did something happen?"

"I was fired," she squeaked out, her throat tightening with emotion.

"Are you serious right now? Mrs. Lamour fired you?"

She forced a nod. "She said someone called her yesterday to complain about how she favors her son over her employees."

"What does that have to do with you?"

"That's what I said," she cried. "Apparently, they traced the area code back to Vermont, and Rodney mentioned that it could have been Elliot."

"Oh no." A deep frown etched into Levi's face. "What if it was?"

"It couldn't have been. He wouldn't do that to me, especially after our conversation yesterday."

"How can you be sure? You only know so much about

the guy."

She rested her hands on her desk to steady herself. "You're right. I don't know him as well as someone I might have hung out with in the real world. But after everything we've discussed, all the secrets we've shared over the last two and a half years . . . I just can't see him breaking my trust like that."

"I sure hope he didn't, for your sake. But what will you do if you find out it was him?"

She gritted her teeth. "What I'd do to anyone in a situation like this. I'd tell him to leave me alone, and I'd never talk to him again. Maybe even change my number."

"Sounds good to me." Levi bowed his head to meet Autumn's eyes, giving her a sympathetic smile. "Maybe this whole thing is for the best."

"I mean, I guess. I just wanted to do it on my own terms—not getting fired," she said, her chest tight as she let out a short huff of exasperation. "I wasn't ready."

"That makes perfect sense." Levi slowly scanned the cluttered office and asked, "Want some help clearing out your stuff?"

"You probably have work to do."

"Come on. My best friend just got fired because of something stupid. The least I can do is help her out. Plus, it won't be long until I turn in that resignation letter of mine."

With that, they started cleaning her office, placing her personal things into cardboard boxes she'd be taking home. All her other unwanted knickknacks and old project sketches got tossed into the mesh trash can at the foot of her desk. As she gathered a sheaf of printouts and stuffed them in the trash, Autumn once again wondered whether Elliot was involved in this debacle. She'd confessed all her work problems to him in confidence, assuming he'd keep those details to himself. But if he really was the culprit who had blabbed to her boss, she doubted she could ever forgive him.

After stepping into the foyer of her home with armfuls of overstuffed boxes, the realization finally sank in. She was now jobless, and she'd need to start from scratch at a new workplace. She dropped her belongings on her off-white coffee table and plopped onto the couch, curling up and hugging her knees to her chest. One by one, warm tears began to drain from her eyes, running down her cheeks and dropping onto the light fabric of her slacks. Autumn didn't know how long she sat there crying to herself, but time felt irrelevant now that everything she worked for had been ripped away in a matter of minutes.

She drew a few shaky breaths to calm herself down, knowing that this wasn't the end of the world, even though it felt like her own personal apocalypse. The one thought that kept pricking at her mind was whether Elliot had played a role in her getting fired. Sick of pondering over the mystery, Autumn picked up her phone, wondering whether she should call him or FaceTime him. She decided she wanted to see his face, especially if this was the last time they spoke. Of course, that would all depend on what answers he gave her.

When she pressed call, it didn't take long for Elliot to

pick up. From the background, she guessed, he was in his office at the café. She had only seen him there once, but the dimly lit confines definitely didn't resemble his home, so his office was her best guess. He smiled, but the joyful expression was soon wiped from his face as he probably noticed her own forlorn appearance.

"What happened?" he asked.

"Did you call my boss?" is all she could say. She chose to be blunt, desperate to know the truth before getting sucked into any type of conversation.

"I . . ." His eyes were wide, his mouth slightly agape as he seemed lost for words. Finally, his head dropped, and he gave her a somber nod. "I did."

"You got me fired," she snapped through gritted teeth. "I wanted all of this to happen on my own terms. Not yours."

"I didn't mean for this to happen," he pleaded, "but your heart seemed bound to that company even as they belittled you, abused you. So, I thought I could help make things a little better there if your boss knew the truth."

"She already knew what was happening, but she refused to acknowledge it. What made you think a random outsider was going to change her mind?"

His face fell as his blue eyes glistened. "Autumn, I'm sorry. I just wanted to help."

"Yeah, well, thanks a lot," Autumn growled, her eyes burning from the tears she was holding back. "Now I'm unemployed and have to figure out my next move sooner rather than later. I don't know if I want to move to Vermont. I don't even know if it's still on the table."

"Why do I get the feeling that this will be our last phone

call," Elliot murmured, almost in a whisper.

Through the pixelated screen, she could see the pain swimming behind his eyes, and she could feel an ache deep down inside her own heart. But what he'd done to her outweighed those feelings. He'd crossed a line. She was hurt, and she didn't think she could maintain a friendship with him without an undertone of resentment, at least not anytime in the near future. After a short pause, she announced bitterly, "I think it is."

A silence stretched between them until Elliot heaved a sigh. "I don't blame you. I'd probably feel the same way if this situation was reversed." Elliot ran a hand through his hair, brushing a few locks out of place. Glancing at his phone's camera, he looked into her eyes one last time. "Goodbye, Autumn."

"Goodbye, Elliot."

With those words, she hung up the call. The unshed tears poured from her eyes as all of her emotions crashed into her in waves. Not only had she lost her job, she'd lost the man she thought she loved. Her life was suddenly at a standstill, and as she huddled on the couch racked with sobs, she had no idea what was next for her.

Chapter 19

Elliot

December 19th

A week had passed since Elliot's final chat with Autumn. He couldn't help but check his phone to see whether she may have changed her mind, but he knew he'd screwed up big time. He wanted to call her, but he figured it'd be best to let her make that decision since the blame lay squarely on his shoulders. He also didn't want to make her any angrier, even if he obviously didn't have a chance at getting her back. But no matter how hard he tried, he couldn't get her off his mind.

For the seventh time today, he was on his phone, staring at her contact page as he wondered whether he should just delete it or continue to hold on to a faint hope that she'd grace him with another phone call. As he bent over the café's front counter, propped on his elbows with the device in hand, Astrid walked up to him. She careened over the counter next to him and asked, "Burn a hole into that thing yet?"

Elliot shot her a glare. "Not yet."

"Do you really think she'll call you after what you did?"

"No. But here's to hoping, right?"

Astrid let out a puff of air through pursed lips. "Maybe she'll surprise you. I mean, Christmas is coming up, and you know what they say. Miracles happen every year."

Elliot groaned as he dropped his head into his hand, his elbow still propped up on the counter. "I doubt a miracle would be wasted on me."

"Don't sell yourself short," Astrid said as she patted his back. "So you did one stupid thing in your thirty-three years on this planet. I think it gets canceled out by all the good you've done, like keeping your dad's shop up and running."

"Well, I'll keep that in mind, but I won't be surprised if I have coal in my stocking this year."

"Could use it with the winter we've been having," she chuckled before strolling away and meandering toward the back of the café.

As Elliot continued to stare at his phone screen, the bell on the door chimed. He looked up to see Sophia walking up to the counter. He gave her a friendly smile and said, "Haven't seen you for a while. How's married life?"

"Not so bad. We had a lovely honeymoon in Bermuda, and we're thinking about trying for a baby," she said, placing her black purse on the counter.

"That sounds great. How has the espresso machine been treating you?"

"It's wonderful. That's why I haven't been in as much, besides being swamped at work."

He chuckled. "I should have given you something else. Now I'm down to four regulars instead of five."

"I'll pop in more often, because nothing is as good as the coffee here." She grazed her fingers over his hand and asked, "Hey, how's that girl you've been talking to?"

He hung his head as he let out a disappointed sigh. "I ruined things with her."

"Oh no, Elliot. You seemed so happy whenever you talked about her. What happened?"

After a moment's hesitation, he explained what he had done, and she audibly gasped as he finished his story. He concluded with, "I don't think she'll speak to me ever again. I don't blame her, either."

Sophia frowned as her warm eyes bored into Elliot. "I agree that what you did was awful. But if she really liked you, she'd forgive you for what you have done and look past this one mistake."

He felt a flutter of hope as he raised his head. "You think so?"

"It's hard to say, but if it were me, I'd give you another chance."

"Thank you." Tearing his gaze away from hers, Elliot turned to the coffee maker and asked, "Do you want your usual?"

"Yes, please."

He started the espresso machine and powered up the frothing wand as he whipped up her order, knowing it like the back of his hand. He placed the steaming cup in front of her, and she started to take out her pocketbook to pay. He waved his left hand and shook his head. "No need. It's on the house."

She huffed, her shoulders sagging slightly. "Are you sure?"

"Yes, I'm positive. I'm feeling generous today."

Sophia grinned. "Well, if this girl doesn't snatch you up, I'm sure someone will. You're a great guy, Elliot." She picked up her purse again, grabbing her coffee and giving a slight wave as she walked to the door. "See you later. And good luck with your lady."

He waved back before returning his attention to his phone. He wasn't holding out hope that he'd receive a phone call from Autumn this Christmas, but there was always a sliver of a chance. He only hoped that sliver was enough to surprise him in the upcoming weeks. If not, he'd just have to move on and hope he could find that happiness once again.

Chapter 20

Autumn

December 19ᵗʰ

Autumn lay back on her bed, staring at the ceiling. She couldn't move from her spot, still wallowing about her job loss, and losing Elliot too. Her eyes stung after all the crying she'd been doing for the past six days. She hadn't showered, or even left the house. Just laid around, shuffling between the bed and the couch like a zombie. As she fell back into her well of pity, her cell phone rang from her nightstand. She picked up the device to check who was calling, thinking it'd be Levi. But it was her sister, Jillian. She hesitated but figured Jill would keep calling if she didn't answer, so she picked up on the third ring. "Hi, Jill."

"You sound awful. Are you sick?" her older sister asked on the other end.

Unable to muster any fake cheer, she said bluntly, "I lost my job."

"How? You've been there so long."

Autumn told her what happened, and at the end of her long-winded explanation, said, "I just can't believe he'd do that to me."

"Me either," Jillian agreed. She exhaled softly on the other end. "What if this is for the best?"

"Maybe, but it's hard to see a light at the end of the tunnel right now."

"You told me you had a job offer in Vermont, right?"

"Sure, but that was five months ago. It's probably long gone by now."

"You don't know if you don't try. Give that agency a call and see if the position is still available."

Autumn draped her free arm over her forehead, studying her light fixture. "I guess it couldn't hurt."

"Hey, I actually called you for a reason." She heard her sister shift her position. "I was hoping you'd come visit us here in Vermont."

"I don't think I'm up for it, Jill," Autumn said as she sat up in her bed.

"Please, I'd love to see you, and you don't have work as an excuse this year."

She groaned quietly. "I'll think about it, but why do you want me to come visit so bad all of a sudden?"

"Well, I was going to wait until you arrived. I told Mom already, so I guess you should know."

"Know what?" she asked, perking up.

"Andy and I are expecting a little girl next year."

A rush of excitement temporarily replaced Autumn's melancholy. "Whoa, congrats! I'm so happy for you two."

"Yes, we can't wait."

"Is that why you want me to move there? Free babysitting, huh?" She chuckled for the first time in the last six days.

"Not really, but if you're offering . . ."

Autumn drew a deep breath, glancing around her messy room. "Maybe I will drop by. I need to get out of the apartment."

"Fantastic. I'll tell Andy to set the guest room up for you." She could practically hear the grin on her sister's face. And honestly, she was happy she'd agreed to drop by. "See you soon," Jillian continued, "Let me know when you fly in."

"I'll share my plans with you soon."

As soon as they said their goodbyes, a knock sounded on her front door. With a grunt, she hauled herself out of her bed and trudged to the door to see who it was. When she opened it a crack, she found Levi standing in front of her with grocery bags in hand. He grimaced as he looked her over and said, "Honey, you look terrible."

"Thank you, Levi. I feel just as bad as I look," she replied, pinching her lips together.

"Well, get ready to cheer up, because I brought us some junk food, margaritas, and boxed wine."

He walked in, setting all the bags onto her kitchen island. Closing the door, she stepped over to him and said, "I'm not really in the mood to hang out."

"I'm sure you will be after we've downed a few glasses of chardonnay." He pulled out some of the food and drinks from the bags. "So, why don't you take a quick shower and put on some comfy clothes, and we can get this pity party started."

She sighed in resignation, rolling her eyes. "All right. I know you won't take no for an answer anyway."

"Nope. I'll start making our drinks meanwhile."

Autumn stole away into her bedroom to get freshened up for her mini bash with Levi. She still wasn't feeling up to it, but maybe it would help her relax—and figure out her next step in life.

December 20th

Autumn and Levi wound up sipping margaritas and chatting way later than she expected. She didn't even remember the last time she'd stayed up past midnight. Their party-of-two sure did help elevate her mood, especially after Levi told her his own plans. He'd already put in his two weeks' notice and signed up for his fashion design classes for next year. His excitement for this new chapter made her realize that maybe she didn't have anything to worry about. Maybe finding design work in Vermont was her new calling. It was still a life in which she could achieve her dream, just a bit different from how she thought it would turn out. As long as she was doing what she loved, it shouldn't matter where she was working and how far behind she was. Even an entry-level position would be better than nothing.

The next morning, with more pep than she had in the last few days, Autumn found the card that Mr. Cardoza had given her. Feeling a prick of anxiety that his offer was off the table, and she'd be turned down for the job, she gathered up her courage and dialed the number on his card. It rang for a few moments before a young man's voice echoed through the speaker. "Mr. Cardoza's office. How can I help you today?"

"My name is Autumn Burke. I'd like to talk with Mr. Cardoza about a job opportunity he offered me," she ventured.

"I don't know if he's taking any calls at this time. At least those that involve job openings."

"Can you mention it to him? Please."

After a brief silence, he said, "Hold on. Let me talk to him."

Once he put her on hold, the only sound filling her ears was boring elevator music that was turned up way too loud. She waited patiently on her couch, hoping that Mr. Cardoza remembered her name and would at least spare her a few minutes of his time. She didn't have to wait much longer when the male receptionist got back on the phone. "Good news, he'll speak with you. I'll patch you through."

The phone rang a few times before being picked up once again, this time by Mr. Cardoza. "Autumn Burke. The one from the banquet, right?"

"That would be me," she said, relieved he remembered her. "I was wondering if you still had a spot in your new Vermont location?"

"You're in luck, because I do have a few more openings

to spare. But I thought you were keen on staying with Mrs. Lamour."

She cleared her throat. "After some recent events, my time at her company has come to a prompt end."

"Ah, sorry to hear that. I have a feeling Rodney was part of the problem."

"He was definitely a factor."

Mr. Cardoza hummed. "Well, after seeing your work over the summer, I think you deserve a spot on my team. We don't open until mid-January, so that should give you time to work things out."

Autumn was speechless. Finally, she stammered, "So, I got the job?"

"Not so fast. I'm not saying it's guaranteed, but there's a very high chance. I just need you to send over your resume and examples of other projects you worked on while at Mrs. Lamour's business." She heard keyboard typing on the other end of the line before he said, "I'll send you back over to my assistant, and he'll give you my email."

"Thank you so much, Mr. Cardoza," Autumn said, feeling light with relief.

"Not a problem. Between you and me, it was her loss, and hopefully my gain. I'm excited to have you work with me. Talk to you soon, Ms. Burke."

The call was bounced back to the receptionist, who gave her Mr. Cardoza's email address so she could send in the pertinent information. She felt like she might float right off her couch, happy that everything seemed to be working out despite the awful week behind her. Now she had to book her flight to Vermont. Luckily, she'd be staying at her sister's house, so she wouldn't have to worry about finding a last-minute hotel smack in the middle of the holiday season. Speaking of which, she had to start planning her move over there, but all that could wait, at least until after Christmas.

Chapter 21

Elliot

December 22nd

Elliot was climbing out of his car to have dinner at Angela's house, but he still had Autumn on his brain twenty-four seven. Nothing he did could shake off his thoughts of her, no matter how hard he tried. It had been ten days, and he was losing hope that she'd ever call him again. Christmas was only a few days away, but he doubted he'd receive that special phone call this year. He was itching to call her, but he didn't want to come off as desperate . . . or worse, a pushy jerk who wouldn't leave her alone. She already had one of those in her life, and that was more than enough. Still, the conundrum he had found himself in was a nightmare. Then again, maybe he deserved it.

After knocking on Angela's front door, he was taken aback when an older man opened it. The man was a few inches shorter than him, with mid-length brown hair peppered with gray strands. His short beard matched his hair but with a little more gray. Elliot glanced around the surrounding neighborhood and said, "I think I got the wrong house."

The man chuckled and then drawled in a thick French accent, "You must be Elliot. Your sister said you'd be coming."

Elliot gaped back. "Are you Remy?"

"Oui, that would be me."

His surprise turned to merriment, and he smiled. "Wow, I didn't realize you'd be in town."

"Your sister didn't either. I wanted to surprise her." Remy motioned for him to come inside and said, "Come, Come."

Elliot stepped inside and found his sister cooking in the kitchen. Remy trailed behind him and announced, "Your brother is here."

Angela looked up, a bright smile that he rarely saw shining on her face. "Elliot, can you believe it?"

"No, I can't," he answered. "I bet it was a nice surprise for you."

"You have no idea."

He turned to the man standing next to him. "How long are you going to stay, Remy?"

Remy shrugged. "For a couple of weeks. As a photographer, I can choose my own vacation time. And

I've been working non-stop for many years; I think I could use a short holiday."

Elliot nodded. "I hope you enjoy your time here."

"It's a lovely place from what I've seen so far. Almost like a storybook. I can't wait to take some photographs while I am here."

Elliot grinned, amused by Remy's childlike wonder. "I'm sure Angela will show you all the wonderful spots here in Shadow Birch."

She nodded as she washed her hands at the sink. "I sure will. There are some wonderful hidden gems that only locals know about."

"I can't wait," Remy said as he cast her a smile.

"So, have you heard anything from Autumn yet?" Angela asked Elliot, crossing her arms in front of her.

Elliot's mood plummeted. "No, and I doubt I will," he replied, wishing she hadn't brought it up.

Remy chimed in, "Autumn is the telephone girl, right?"

Elliot's eyes shot to his sister, his eyebrows arching. "You told him?"

Angela waved it off. "What? We talk a lot. It was bound to come up during one of our conversations."

He turned to Remy, admitting, "Yes, that's her. I accidently got her fired, and now she hates my guts. She never wants to speak to me again."

"That's too bad," Remy said with an expression of sympathy. "You should give her a call. You seem remorseful enough."

"I agree," Angela interjected.

A sigh left Elliot's lips, "I thought about it. I could always call her on Christmas, like usual. If she doesn't pick up, then I guess I'll have my answer."

Angela nodded her approval. "That sounds like a good idea. I mean, it's worth a shot, right?"

"Absolutely." Elliot stole a glance toward the stovetop, where a covered dish sat. "What's for dinner?"

Angela gestured to the dish and said, "Ratatouille, in honor of Remy being here."

"Did you make it yourself?" Elliot asked and grimaced at the thought. "No offense sis, but I know for a fact your cooking skills are minuscule."

She rolled her eyes. "Remy helped me some."

Remy nodded and added, "Your sister did a great job, though. She only needed a little bit of guidance."

"Well, I hope we're not all rushed to the hospital tonight for potential food poisoning."

She threw a dishrag square at his chest. "Hush, you!"

Remy chortled briefly and said, "You two remind me of my younger brother and me. We don't have such a big age gap as you two, only five years, but we'd bicker all the time."

"Is he your only sibling?" Elliot asked.

Remy studied the floor. "We had an older brother, but he died several years ago due to health complications."

"Sorry to hear that."

"Thank you. We weren't as close, but we all miss him dearly."

Angela grabbed the porcelain dish from the stove with two potholders in her hands and carried it over to her six-seater dining table that was lightly decorated with a poinsettia-print table runner and an antique candelabra. She took a seat, peered back at the two men, and said,

"Why don't we start eating before it gets cold?"

They sat down to join her and dug into a dinner that was tender and flavorful despite Elliot's worries about Angela's notoriously bad cooking skills. They talked and laughed as they finished off several helpings of ratatouille, and Elliot had a great time getting to know Remy beyond what Angela had told him. As he watched the two joke and smile throughout the night, he was once again surprised that they weren't together. But he didn't want to pry into Angela's relationship, especially since he'd asked her not to pry into his. Still, they'd make a cute couple, even if it took them more than a decade to get there.

Their riveting evening even got his mind off Autumn for a short while, until some phrase or story reminded him of her, making him keenly aware of that ache in his chest. Beyond his lingering heartache, Elliot felt like a kid again, anxiously waiting for Christmas to arrive. But not because Santa was coming. He was desperate to give Autumn a call, even though he feared that it'd be a lost cause and he'd have to return to his life before Autumn. And honestly, that life wasn't that great.

Chapter 22

Autumn

December 24th

Autumn was curled up on her sister's couch as she sipped hot chocolate with mini marshmallows served in an oversized red mug. She pulled the fluffy blanket further over her as she watched a cheesy holiday romance movie on the big-screen TV. She'd been about to change the channel when it came on about an hour ago, but she got so invested in the predictable storyline and cliché characters that she ended up watching it. She couldn't believe that the lead woman was trying so hard to win her ex-boyfriend back when her best friend was clearly in love with her—and a nicer guy than the jerk of an ex. She tsked at the screen as the woman tried to flirt with her ex again before a commercial came on. Taking a sip of her now lukewarm drink, she sank further into the couch and waited for the movie to come back on.

Jillian walked into the room with, an arm full of presents of varying sizes. She unloaded and arranged them all under the Christmas tree by the fireplace before joining her sister on the couch. Jill patted the blanket swaddling Autumn's legs and said, "When I invited you to stay with us for the holidays, I didn't think you'd be sitting around moping the whole time."

"What am I supposed to be doing? There's not much for entertainment around here," Autumn answered.

"I don't know. Take a look around the town, see the sights, get some fresh air."

"It's too cold out there, and I'm content right here."

Jillian gave her an exasperated look. "Come on. You should be thrilled that you're going to be moving here and working under a way better boss than your old one."

"I am thrilled," Autumn responded, sitting up and setting her empty mug onto the coffee table. "It's just going to be hard for me to adjust to this sudden change."

"But people do it all the time."

"I know, but some people handle it better than others."

"I see your point." Jillian wrapped a thin arm around Autumn, pulling her into a side embrace. "Why do I get the feeling this isn't really about your upcoming move?"

Autumn released a long sigh.

"You still have that Elliot guy on the brain."

She nodded, dropping her head in her hands. "He probably never wants to speak to me again."

"From what you told me, *you're* the one who made the call to never talk to him again."

"I did, but I'm sure he's deleted my contact and expunged me from his memory by now."

A mischievous glint came to Jillian's eyes. "There's only one way to find out."

Autumn glared back. "I'm not going to call him."

"Who said anything about calling?"

Autumn sat back; her eyebrows knitted together as she puzzled over what her sister could be suggesting. "Are you saying what I think you're saying?"

Jill shrugged. "If it's to go see him in person, then yeah, that's exactly what I'm saying."

Her heart thumped at the thought. "Oh no, I can't meet him in person."

"Why not?"

"I just can't. I don't even know where his café is."

Jill brought out her phone from her pocket and said, "I'm sure we can find it."

"No, I can't see him. Not after everything that happened," Autumn blurted as she tried to grab the phone from her sister.

Jillian's playful expression fell. "Do you really want to live your life never knowing if you were meant to be together? Just because there was a small hiccup in the relationship doesn't mean you should let it go without a fight."

Autumn scoffed. "I mean, it's better than getting rejected, right?"

Jillian gave her a pointed look. "Not in my opinion. If I had hung onto the time that Andy didn't call me for a whole week and forgot to pick me up at the airport back in college, then we wouldn't be here today expecting our little girl. And if I remember correctly, a certain someone told me to give him another chance."

Autumn blushed as she stared down at her hands. "You think I should?"

"I do. If it doesn't work out, then I give you permission to say 'told you so' and nag me every Christmas season about it."

Autumn gathered her last ounce of courage and said, "Okay, let's see if we can find him."

With a victorious grin, Jill went into the map app on her phone to find Elliot's café. She hit the search bar and asked, "Do you know the name of the café by any chance?"

"I think it started with an L." Autumn wracked her brain to recall what he had told her. "'Law' something."

"Lawson's Bistro?" Jillian asked, not looking up from her phone.

"I think that's it."

"Then you're in luck because it's in Shadow Birch. That's the next town over. Only a fifteen-minute drive to get there."

Autumn snatched the phone from Jillian, marveling at the red marker pointing to Elliot's café. She was right. It was indeed only fifteen minutes away from her sister's house. Autumn had been secretly hoping it was much farther so she didn't have to go. But now she would have to keep her word and see him so her sister would leave her alone about it. Andy soon returned from his run to the grocery store, and Jillian got off the couch, her small baby bump showing slightly as she rose. She planted a kiss on her husband's lips. "I know you just got home, but I need you to go out again."

"What are you craving? I tried to get lots of options, but I can go back out," he stuttered as he tried to rifle through the handful of bags he was carrying.

"No, I'm fine. This is a trip for Autumn."

He glanced between them. "Where to?"

"You know the phone guy she's been talking to? We found where he works, and she's going to pay him a visit."

"Nice," he said, shooting Autumn a smile. "But can I put the groceries away first?"

"Yes, I'll help you." Jillian turned to her sister and said, "You get dressed, and we'll leave when we're done."

Before Autumn could object, Jill and Andy were ambling toward the kitchen. She sighed, a nervous bug creeping up on her as she dragged herself off the couch. She wasn't sure if she was ready to finally meet Elliot in person, especially after everything that had happened. Would he even be excited to see her? Whatever the case, she was going to find out soon enough.

They were pulled up next to a flower shop a couple of stores down from the café. Autumn's leg wouldn't stop bouncing up and down as she fidgeted with the wool gloves on her hands. Jill craned her neck to face her from the passenger seat. "You have to go in sometime."

"Maybe we should just go back to your place and forget about this whole thing," Autumn said with a shrug.

Jillian looked aghast, her jaw dropping. "No way! We

did not come all this way for you to chicken out."

"I can't do this. What if he's not even the one for me?"

"But what if he is?"

She stared down at her gloves for a moment. "Then I guess I'll never know."

Jill frowned before turning to Andy in the driver's seat. "Why don't we cause a little ruckus by blaring the horn a bit?"

Autumn lunged forward in her seat, gripping Andy's right arm. "No, there's no need for that."

"Then go see your man," Jill said with her left eyebrow raised. "Or you leave us no choice."

"I'll go, I'll go," she relented with a huff. "There's no need to fight dirty."

Autumn stepped out of the car, feeling the soft and cold flakes of the light snow melt as they hit her face. She marched in the direction of Elliot's café, getting cold feet with each step she took—and not from the weather. When she reached the storefront window that bore the café's name and logo, she peered in, searching for him. She caught a glimpse of the chiseled jaw she had only seen through FaceTime only a few feet away from her. He was talking to a woman with red hair, who was hanging out behind the counter with him. She guessed it was one of his employees because she was wearing an apron in the same shade as the light-yellow logo out front.

Autumn slinked away, hoping Elliot hadn't noticed her. He did seem a bit preoccupied, so she was sure she was in the clear. She leaned up against the brick wall next to the café and fished out her phone from the pocket of her gray coat. Gazing down at the number she still kept on her phone, she contemplated whether she should call him or just walk in. As she tried to make a decision, her sister made one for her by honking the horn in three short bursts. She whipped her head toward the commotion, glaring toward the car, where she could vaguely see her sister gesturing for her to go inside. She groaned, turning toward the café, but instead ran into the chest of a man. Her phone dropped to the ground at the sudden impact, and the man wasted no time in retrieving it for her. When he stood, their eyes met, and her heart leaped. The snowfall seemed to halt, suspended in midair as she stared into the eyes of the man she had only seen on a tiny screen.

Elliot looked to be in pure shock, his lower jaw hanging slightly open and his blue eyes wide. "Au. . . Autumn?"

"It's nice to finally see you in person," she whispered.

"You're really here? This isn't a dream?"

"No, this is very much real."

"I thought you were mad at me," he said, looking hurt.

"I was beyond mad." She sighed, offering him a hint of a smile. "But you tried to help me when I was stuck in a bad place, doing nothing, and honestly, it was for the better." Autumn looked up at Elliot, her nervous smile widening. "So, you're not mad at *me*?"

"Why would I be? I was the one who almost screwed up your entire life."

She shuffled her feet on the snow-glazed sidewalk. "For being stupid, I guess. Not taking your opinion, along with my best friend's, to have left that place sooner."

His gaze burned into her. "I'd never be mad at you for that. You had valid reasons to not rock the boat, and you needed time to see it through. You shouldn't have been forced into it, and for that I'm sorry."

She shook her head. "You don't need to apologize, Elliot. None of that matters anymore, and I'm happy it all went down the way it did."

He blinked back at her, snowflakes catching on his brown hair. "So, are you moving to Vermont?"

"I am." She smiled as she kicked the packed snow with the tips of her black boots. "I'll be finding my own place soon and starting my new job with Mr. Cardoza next year."

With no warning, Elliot pulled her into a hug before promptly pulling away, biting his bottom lip. "Sorry about that."

She giggled, her heart fluttering. "Don't be. I've been waiting for this since our second conversation."

As their eyes met again, the gentle snowfall enveloping them in their own magic world, Elliot bent down, capturing Autumn's lips with his. She didn't pull away as they shared their first kiss, the warmth and passion melting her heart. When they pulled away, Autumn could feel her cheeks burning despite the biting chill in the air. Elliot smiled down at her and said, "And I've been waiting to do that since our *first* conversation."

Breaking herself out of her trance, Autumn smiled back and asked, "Are you doing anything tomorrow?"

"On Christmas . . . I usually have a date with a certain caller from across the country, but I think she'll understand."

"I think she'll let this one Christmas slide," she murmured. "I heard she had plans anyway."

He chuckled before placing another kiss on her lips. A

long honk broke them apart as Jillian and Andy pulled up next to them. Elliot looked over to the car and asked, "Do you know them?"

"Unfortunately, I do. That's my sister and her husband. They brought me here today," Autumn answered, wiping her left hand down her flustered cheek.

"Oh," Elliot said as he gave a brief wave toward the car. "My sister probably would have done the same."

She turned back to him. "So, you'll come over to my sister's house for Christmas tomorrow?"

"Of course. Uh, do you mind if I bring my sister along, and her friend from France?"

Autumn didn't even get to answer before her sister called out from the window, "The more the merrier. We have plenty of room."

"Thank you," he called back.

"I'll text you the address then," Autumn said as she looked down at the phone still clutched in Elliot's hand.

"Sounds good," he said, still not realizing her phone was with him.

"I kind of need my phone to do that," she giggled.

"Oh, sorry. I completely forgot." He handed the device back over and said, "So, I'll see you tomorrow then?"

She nodded, a swell of happiness filling her chest. "See you then."

"Wait." Before she could step away, Elliot grabbed Autumn's forearm. "Do we have to wait until tomorrow? I'd love to show you around Shadow Birch."

"She'd love to," Jill butted in.

"I can speak for myself, thanks," Autumn said, shooting Jillian an annoyed glance before turning back to Elliot.

"I'd like that."

He nodded to her sister and said, "I promise I won't keep her out too late."

Jillian swatted her hand toward them. "Go ahead and keep her for as long as you'd like. She deserves to have some fun."

Jillian waved goodbye with a cheeky smile as Andy drove off. Once their car had disappeared down the road, Elliot looked down at Autumn, a kind smile brightening his face in the snowy night. "Would you like to see my café? Maybe you can give me a few decorating pointers. The theme this year is 'winter wonderland,' and I'm kind of out of ideas."

"Sure, and don't worry. I'll make sure not to critique it too harshly," she snickered as he led her to the entrance.

He joined her in laughter. "Go ahead, I can take it."

They stepped inside, where Autumn was introduced to Elliot's employee Astrid as he gave her the grand tour of the café. She was actually pretty impressed with the small shop all decked out for the holidays—and the charming town it resided in. She would have never expected this, but Autumn had a feeling she was going to enjoy her time here in Vermont. Beyond that, she was excited to see what was in store in her new life, especially if she had Elliot by her side.

Epilogue

Autumn peered out the open window of the hotel room, a fresh breeze was blowing against her face as she gazed up at the Eiffel Tower that stood only a few blocks from where they were staying. As she took in the stunning sight a strong pair of arms wrapped around her midsection, pulling her into a warm embrace. Elliot nuzzled his face into the crook of her neck, his stubble tickling her skin. As he rested there, he mumbled, "We're going to be late for my sister's wedding."

Turning in his arms and slipping her arms around his neck, she glanced up at his crystal blue eyes. "You're the one who spent a half-hour on your bowtie."

"I wanted to make sure it looked presentable."

"It's still crooked," she chuckled as she adjusted the maroon-colored bowtie against his neck.

"At least I can tie it now. Years ago, I could barely even form the first fold."

She messed with the tie a bit more and observed her work. "Maybe you'll get it perfected by the time our wedding comes around."

"Our wedding?" he asked, his left brow raised and a hint of a smirk tugging at his lips.

Autumn felt her face flush, not realizing what she'd said until now. It's not like they hadn't talked about their future, but never so casually like she had just now. "Well, I mean there might be. You know . . . We probably have a while until then."

He kissed her pouty lips, stopping her rambling. She relaxed into his tender touch, and once he pulled away from her, he said, "I'm sure it won't be long."

Her cheeks heated up once again in learning that he shared her sentiments. That they could be walking down that aisle sometime soon, and part of her couldn't wait for that day to come. Elliot peeked down at the watch on his wrist as he gently pulled away from Autumn. "We should head downstairs before it gets too late."

"Let's get going," she said, hooking her arm inside the crook of Elliot's left elbow.

The two headed out of the hotel room and into the elevator. Elliot pressed the glossy button to the first floor, and the antiquated contraption slowly descended. Autumn heard her phone vibrate in her maroon clutch that matched her dress. She pulled it out and was greeted with a message from Jillian, which included a new photo of her niece. She brought it up for Elliot to see. "Ella started kindergarten today."

"Aww, she looks so cute. I know we saw her a couple of weeks ago, but I could swear she's grown since then," he said as he smiled down at the picture.

"They grow fast, don't they? It feels like she was just born."

"Crazy . . . Five years. Almost as long as we've been together, if you don't count our first phone call."

Her eyes wandered around the elevator and settled on Elliot. "Who would have thought a random call would lead to all of this?"

"Not me," he answered. "But I sure am glad I decided not to throw away that old rotary from my great-grandmother. Who knows where we'd be now?"

She sighed. "I'd still probably be at my old office, a workaholic, with only Levi to keep me company."

Thinking back, Autumn recalled reading an article from a renowned decorating magazine that the Lamours were wrapped up in quite the scandal. Rodney had shamelessly plagiarized a fellow decorator's design, only this time, the other designer had the original drafts and was able to prove Rodney stole them. Mrs. Lamour defended her son, of course, but she doubted Rodney would ever be accepted in the design world again.

"And now you're one of interior decorating's rising stars on the East Coast," he added with a look of pride. "Well, I'd still be running the café like I am now, but with way less enthusiasm. Hating Christmas, and possibly going down a dark path that I don't even want to think about."

She swung to face him, her brow furrowed. "Do you

think it was fate?"

"Hmm . . ." He pinched at his bottom lip, his face scrunching in uncertainty as he thought about it. "I was never one to believe in fate or soulmates. But after everything that happened between us, and the way everything seemed to fall into place, maybe it was."

"I'm starting to believe something brought us together, and I'm happy that it did."

"I couldn't agree more," he said, planting a kiss on her cheek.

The elevator doors opened, and they headed to the room where the ceremony would be held. When they got to the double doors of the entrance, Remy sauntered over to them with a chipper smile. "Bonjour, Elliot and Autumn. You both look *très magnifique* this afternoon."

"Thank you, Remy. You don't look half-bad yourself," Elliot replied as he gestured to the man's tailored tuxedo.

"Merci." Remy gestured toward the small room that was quickly filling with a handful of guests as the ceremony drew near. "We're just about to begin. Your sister should be finishing up."

Elliot nodded. "I'll go find her and get ready to walk her down the aisle."

"Great. I'll go talk to the priest and get in position."

Remy jogged away, greeting a few other guests as he made his way to the altar. Elliot peered down at Autumn and said, "You're sure that you're fine with walking down the aisle with Remy's brother, Théo?"

"Of course! They're all very nice." She rested a hand on Elliot's forearm, adding, "And I know how much this means to you two. I think it'll be sweet for you to give her away. I'd want the same thing if I had a brother, but at least I do have Levi, and he's close enough."

He released the breath he was holding. "I'm glad you understand." With that, he kissed her cheek again before running off to find Angela.

Autumn smiled after him before looking around for Remy's younger brother so they could prepare for the big moment.

After a quick search, Elliot found his sister applying some finishing touches to her light makeup. He entered the tiny side room, trying his best not to step on the lace train of her beautiful eggshell-white gown. He sidled up next to her in the slim mirror and said, "You look lovely, sis."

"And you look as handsome as always, baby brother." Angela placed a sweet peck on his cheek.

"Are you ready?" he asked.

"Yes, but are you?"

"Of course. I'm honored to walk you down the aisle."

"I'm glad about that, but that's not what I was referring to."

"What are you talking about?" he asked, puzzled.

"You and Autumn," she said, enthusiasm laced in her voice. "You brought the ring to Paris, right?"

He nodded, feeling a sudden wave of nerves. "I did. It's currently burning a hole in the side compartment of my carry-on bag."

She stood back, folding her arms over her lace-embroidered bodice. "So, you're going to do it?"

His gaze fell to the floor. "I don't know. I would love to propose to her, but . . ."

"Don't get cold feet on me, Elliot. Propose to the girl you love, and in one of the most romantic cities in the world at that. It'll be spectacular."

"Well, we do have dinner reservations tomorrow at a nice restaurant about an hour from here, since we'll be visiting the Louvre and Notre Dame Cathedral. I was thinking of proposing by the square nearby, since it has a beautiful fountain."

"As your older sister, here's my advice—go for it. Don't wait any longer. You two clearly belong together, so why not make it official like Remy and me?"

"Sure, but you also stated pretty clearly that you had no feelings for him and weren't getting hitched."

"So? Things change. We're all in a happier place now, and why let time slip away?"

"You do have a point." Drawing a breath of confidence and wearing a grin that made his cheeks sore, Elliot announced, "I think I'm going to do it."

"Yes! I can't wait to hear all about it." Angela grabbed her veil, placed it on her head, and said, "But before we can start fantasizing about your future wedding, I need to finish mine."

"You're right. let's get going, shall we?" he asked as he jutted his elbow out for Angela to take.

She laced her arm around her brother's and answered, "We shall."

Elliot led his sister out of the room and toward the entrance of the salon. The wedding planner cued the traditional "Here Comes the Bride" tune to start playing before they started their trek down the aisle. There weren't many attendees, just a handful of friends and family from both sides, so the walk was fairly short. But the whole time as they strode down the aisle, Elliot couldn't take his eyes off Autumn, who was standing dutifully at the front of the altar next to the other two bridesmaids. She looked stunning in her maroon gown, a cheerful smile lighting up her face as her eyes landed on his. He could feel his heart hammering in his chest as he took her in. He was happy, he realized. Happy that they were able to be together.

Elliot handed Angela off to Remy before taking his spot by the groomsmen, standing across from his gorgeous girlfriend. He tried to focus on his sister's ceremony, but all he could think about was the engagement ring back in the hotel room. He couldn't wait to pop the question to Autumn tomorrow, thrilled to start the next chapter of his life with the woman he loved.

<u>Thank you for Reading!</u>

Dear Reader, I hope you've enjoyed reading *The Christmas Calls*. If you have the time, it would be greatly appreciated if you could leave a short review for the book. It doesn't just help the author, but future readers as well, and I'm sure they'd be thankful for it too.
Thank you!

<u>Stay in Touch with Timi Petal</u>

Follow Timi Petal on Facebook and Instagram:
Facebook: https://www.facebook.com/people/Timi-Petal-Romance/100088230609748/
Instagram: @timipetal_romance
Website: https://tprice2author.wixsite.com/timipetal

I sincerely hope you enjoyed reading this book as much as I enjoyed writing it.

About the Author

Timi Petal doesn't actually exist. She's just a pen name for an author who does. Even if she's not necessarily real, the person she embodies likes to think she is, at least somewhat. Timi Petal is the half who loves a good romance novel. Anything sweet or romantic, she is interested.

After many years of watching Hallmark Christmas movies, romantic comedies, and reading sweet romances, Timi Petal decided to dive into the writing world herself. She created her own beloved characters and scenarios that will hopefully make fellow readers' hearts swoon. Her debut holiday romance novel, *The Christmas Calls*, is her first attempt to enter the romance world.

Timi Petal lives in the sunny state of Florida with her family, a fifteen-year-old Pomeranian, and a one-year-old Corgi.